Atlas

WEATHERHEAD BOOKS ON ASIA

WEATHERHEAD EAST ASIAN INSTITUTE,

COLUMBIA UNIVERSITY

Atlas

The Archaeology of an Imaginary City

BY DUNG KAI-CHEUNG

Translated by Dung Kai-cheung, Anders Hansson,
and Bonnie S. McDougall

Columbia University Press
New York

This publication has been supported by the Richard W. Weatherhead Publication
Fund of the Weatherhead East Asian Institute, Columbia University.

Columbia University Press thanks Mr. Zhang Dapeng for his
contribution toward the publication of this book.

Columbia University Press

Publishers Since 1893

New York   Chichester, West Sussex

cup.columbia.edu

First published as *Dituji—yi ge xiangxiang de chengshi de kaoguxue* by the Unitas
Publishing Co., Ltd , Taipei, 1997; revised edition by Linking Publishing Co., Taipei,

2011

Library of Congress Cataloging-in-Publication Data

Dong, Qizhang, 1967–

[Di tu ji. English]

Atlas : the archaeology of an imaginary city / by Dung Kai-cheung ; translated by
Dung Kai-Cheung, Anders Hansson, and Bonnie S. McDougall.

p.   cm.

Includes bibliographical references.

ISBN 978-0-231-16100-8 (cloth : acid-free paper) —

ISBN 978-0-231-50422-5 (electronic)

1. Hong Kong (China)—Fiction. I. Hansson, Anders, 1944-
II. McDougall, Bonnie S., 1941- III. Title.

PL2936.3.O54D52813   20112

895.1′352—dc23   2011035907

Columbia University Press books are printed on permanent and
durable acid-free paper.

This book was printed on paper with recycled content.

Printed in the United States of America

c 10 9 8 7 6 5 4 3 2

For Nim-yan, Sun-gwo,
and Torkel

Contents

PART FOUR: SIGNS

∽

AN ARCHAEOLOGY FOR THE FUTURE

The miracle of Hong Kong is that it has always been evolving, incorporating elements of both Chinese and foreign cultures, accommodating influxes of immigrants from the Chinese mainland in different historical periods, and nevertheless maintaining a distinctive cultural identity. This city of immigrants is also a city of locals. Yet the founding of Hong Kong is a historical accident. Had the British not chosen to occupy the barren northern coast of the island in 1841 and set out to make it a colony, Hong Kong as we know it today would not have existed. There is no need for its present inhabitants to express gratitude for that, but we have to admit to the fact that Hong Kong was invented. It was one of the marvelous inventions in human history. Hong Kong has been a work of fiction from its very beginning.

There are enough fictitious Hong Kongs circulating around the world. It doesn't matter so much how real or false these fictions are but how they are made up. The Hong Kong of Tai-Pan and Suzie Wong, a mixture of economic adventures, political intrigues, sexual encounters, and romances; the Hong Kong of Bruce Lee, Jackie Chan, and Jet Li kung fu fighting their way through to the international scene; the Hong Kong of John Woo's gangster heroes shooting doublehanded and Stephen Chow's underdog antiheroes making nonsensical jokes. And yet, in spite of these eye-catching exposures, Hong Kong remains invisible. A large part of the reality of life here is unrepresented, unrevealed, and ignored. Hong Kong's martial arts fiction, commercial movies, and pop songs are successful in East Asia and even farther abroad, but for all the talents, insights, and creativity of its writers, Hong Kong literature attracts minimal attention—not just internationally but even in mainland China. I am not claiming that literature represents a Hong Kong more real than the movies, but it has its unique role and methods and thus yields different meanings. It is not just a different way of world-representing but also a different way of world-building, that is, creating conditions for understanding, molding, preserving, and changing the world that we live in.

It is the task of literature to make visible the invisible. (Or, as is sometimes said, to articulate the unarticulated.) Curiously, in contrast to visual art forms like film, literature has a special capacity for rendering visibility. Words are nonvisual signs and many steps removed from the actual and the visible. By virtue of this removal, however, words invoke an imaginative power that is not bound by a photographic image. Telling and writing play on the dialectic between the visible and invisible, and that is the true meaning of "making visible." This making is no less than the work of an artisan, in whose hands a world of objects is made and an abode of dwelling is built. What is more, it is not an abode of bricks and tiles but an abode of meanings.

It was in this spirit that I wrote *Atlas*, a verbal collection of maps. It was written and published in 1997, in the year the colony of Hong Kong was returned by its British rulers to become a Special Administrative Region under Chinese sovereignty. Nevertheless I chose not to write directly about the event or the contemporary situation in the narrow sense. The perspective was set in an unknown future time but with a retrospective, archaeological orientation, inquiring into the origin and the long-lost past of the city. The city is supposed to have vanished, and efforts are made by scholars to re-create its history through imaginative readings of maps and documents unearthed only recently. The city is literally rebuilt by relics and fragments, casting a shadow on the question of reality and authenticity and in turn making way for the introduction of fiction into the process of history making.

The claim of history as fiction may seem far-fetched, reductive, and nihilistic, but it has a special applicability to Hong Kong. Hong Kong is often called a borrowed place in a borrowed time. It's a colonial and therefore biased view, but it's not because of any doctrine of national sovereignty that I reject it. This doctrine holds that Hong Kong has never been a colony, since the unequal treaties between the Qing dynasty and the United Kingdom have never been recognized by the People's Republic of China. It also claims that the saying no longer makes sense after Hong Kong's return to its mother country. My rejection is instead from the perspective of a person who grew up in Hong Kong in its last colonial phase and continues to live here in the post-1997 era. I and many others like me simply don't accept this description of the place where we live. Why? It's because we belong to the space-time that is ours. Nobody lends it to us and we don't borrow it from anybody.

I am not arguing for any kind of essentialism, of a pure and original identity that has always been there, static, unchanging, and unchangeable. The idea of "borrowed place" and "borrowed time," if taken positively, can also mean possibilities that have not been realized. It can liberate the borrowed from the lender and the borrower. The borrowed is the space and time, and these two make up the spatial and temporal existence of a people that is authentic and not falsifiable. Paradoxically, such authenticity and unfalsifiability can only be mapped, verified, understood, and pursued

through fiction. Fiction has always been a means of identity building, and the metafiction of a society is an extended and unending
bildungsroman.

This may all sound very functional, even programmatic, but it is
not so. Literature always begins with self-questioning, and to write
is an attempt to answer these doubts. Literary writing remains a
personal matter, with no support from the outside and no collabo-
ration with peers. Yet in writing, we are wonderfully connected in
a common concern, a common care that makes us belong in the
strongest possible sense. It is a new meaning offered by the phrase
"personal belonging," a near oxymoron, joining the private with the
public. *Atlas* is a personal work, with all sorts of idiosyncratic and
wild theories and interpretations, mixing with all sorts of extravagant exercises in imagination and camouflaged insertions of private experiences. Yet *Atlas* is also meant to be a work that belongs.
It testifies to a belonging that was born a long time ago and has
been growing since then, responding to but not determined by outward circumstances, whether political change, social upheaval, or
economic disaster.

Belonging never closes off possibilities, it is rather the condition for possibilities. It makes possible. Space and time can never
be borrowed, nor can they be returned. As one, as space and time
should be, it can only belong, and can only belong to a certain people (or peoples). Belonging is always common, but it is also always
multiple. That is why I would never take *Atlas* as a conclusion or
ending of a historical period specific to Hong Kong but as the starting point for historical narratives, or histories, that open to us not
only the path to the past but also the way to the future. It is in this
sense that *Atlas* can be an archaeology for the future.

I want to thank Bonnie S. McDougall and Anders Hansson for
their joint efforts in translating *Atlas* into English. Bonnie's skill in

rendering meanings accurately and yet at the same time flexibly is enlightening, and Anders's eye for the precision of details is admirable. I have learned many things from them as a cotranslator and have made revisions to the original Chinese text at various places that couldn't stand the close scrutiny of these two experienced teachers. If there are still any flaws and obscurities in the English text, the responsibility is entirely mine. I would also like to thank David Der-wei Wang, Edward C. Henderson Professor of Chinese Literature in the Department of East Asian Languages and Cultures at Harvard University, for recommending my book to Columbia University Press, as well as the press staff for their efforts in making *Atlas* visible to the English-speaking world.

Dung Kai-cheung

Hong Kong

June 2011

Introduction

1

Dung Kai-cheung's *Atlas* has been compared to Italo Calvino's *Le città invisibili* (*Invisible Cities*);[1] the names Jorge Luis Borges, Umberto Eco, and Roland Barthes also appear in *Atlas* and have been cited as influences. Yet *Atlas*, "a verbal collection of maps," is unique, an extraordinary assemblage of fact and fiction; of history, geography, philosophy, and politics; of imagination and wit; of fantasy and anecdote. It is a novel without a plot; there is a wide range of characters but none dominant; there is sex and violence but all offstage. The profusion of place-names in its early chapters can be daunting, as also the abstract conceptualizations toward its end; but throughout, the author's strange blend of humor and distress infuses his apparent detachment as he re-creates his city's past and present, just as his archaeologist of the future attempts to re-create it through old maps, blueprints, and urban plans.

Dung Kai-cheung has been described as Hong Kong's most accomplished writer. His work has been praised by the eminent literary sinologists Leo Ou-fan Lee and David Der-wei Wang and anthologized in collections of Hong Kong literature. His novels have been published in Hong Kong, Taiwan, and the Chinese mainland, yet they are little known outside Hong Kong and Taiwan.

It has been suggested that Hong Kong lacks the literary identity to be the subject of attention of an international reading public, yet fiction written in English, set in Hong Kong and telling Hong Kong stories, has been consistently popular beyond East Asia. As well as large numbers of crime thrillers and historical romances, there has also been a long string of commercial and critical successes, from Han Suyin's *A Many-Splendoured Thing* (1952) and Richard Mason's *The World of Suzie Wong* (1957; still in print) to John le Carré's *The Honourable Schoolboy* (1977), Timothy Mo's *The Monkey King* (1978), Paul Theroux's *Kowloon Tong* (1997), and John Lanchester's *Fragrant Harbour* (2002). These novelists are outsiders, temporarily resident in Hong Kong. Dung Kai-cheung was born in Hong Kong and has lived there all his life: his personal experience has enlivened his research into the past and given him apprehensive hopes for the future.

2

Dung Kai-cheung (in Mandarin, Dong Qizhang) was born in Hong Kong in 1967. His father had moved from China to the New Territories countryside in Hong Kong and then to Kowloon, where Kai-cheung grew up in the crowded streets of one of the world's most densely populated areas. He received his BA and MPhil in comparative literature at the University of Hong Kong, the colony's first and still most prominent university. He now teaches part-time in several Hong Kong universities but spends most of his time writing novels, short stories, literary criticism, and reviews.

His major works of fiction began to appear in the mid-1990s; eighteen have already been published and more are on the way. The titles of two novels acknowledge two of the writers with whom he has been compared: *The Rose of the Name* (1997) and *Visible Cities*

(1998). *Atlas* is the first of his novels to have been translated into English and has also been translated into Japanese. Another novel, *Works and Creations* (2005), was adapted for the stage and successfully performed in Hong Kong in 2007. His most recent novels are *Histories of Time* (2007) and *The Age of Learning* (2010). Collections of his reviews and literary criticism, two of them coauthored with Wong Nim-yan, were published in 1996, 1997, and 1998; the most recent title is *Writing in the World and for the World* (2011).

Dung Kai-cheung has won literary awards in Taiwan and Hong Kong, including the Unitas Fiction Writing Award for New Writers (1994), the United Daily News Literary Award for the Novel (1995), and the Hong Kong Arts Development Council Literary Award for New Writers (1997). *Works and Creations* received wide critical acclaim and was ranked among the best ten in the Annual Book Awards (2005) of the two major literary supplements in Taiwan (*Unitas Daily* and *China Times Daily*). It also won the Adjudicators' Award, The Dream of Red Chamber Award: The World's Distinguished Novel in Chinese, Hong Kong Baptist University in 2006. *Histories of Time* won the same award in 2008. He received the Award for Best Artist 2007/2008 (literary arts) by the Hong Kong Arts Development Council. In 2009 he spent several months in the International Writing Program at the University of Iowa. Their reputation in Hong Kong and Taiwan firmly established, his works are now being published in mainland China and Japan.

Atlas: The Archaeology of an Imaginary City (in Mandarin, *Dituji: Yi ge xiangxiang de chengshi de kaoguxue*) was first published in Taipei by the Unitas Publishing Company in 1997; a revised version appeared in 2011. It is a fictional account of the City of Victoria (Hong Kong), a legendary city that has disappeared, written from the perspective of future archaeologists who reconstruct the form and facts about the city through imaginative readings of maps and other historical documents. It has fifty-one short chapters grouped into four parts: "Theory," "The City," "Streets," and "Signs." Each chapter is a mixture of fact and fiction, narrative and description. The novel poses questions about the representation of a place and its history through a visual medium that is supposedly scientific and technical: maps. It is about the invention of a city through mapping and its reinvention through map reading. The author takes a distanced view of Hong Kong's colonized past and its sinicized present, employing a range of writing styles to rearrange the two in a fragmented narrative. Interspersed throughout are moments of lyrical recollections of individual experience.

The opening of part 1 may seem intimidating from its title "Theory" to its long list of real and imaginary place-names in the first chapter: even some of the actual place-names are hardly familiar to long-term Hong Kong residents. Nevertheless, the chapter titles, which initially seem ponderously Foucauldian, starting with "Counterplace" and continuing to "Commonplace," hint at playfulness in "Misplace" and "Displace" and end up as mythic with the final six variations, "Utopia," "Supertopia," "Subtopia," "Transtopia," "Multitopia," "Unitopia," and "Omnitopia." The names of Calvino, Eco, Barthes, and Borges in the main text and notes also suggest that a fictional world is being created.

In part 1 we are introduced to a first-person narrator to whom is attributed a wistfulness about the past, especially about old maps and other documents that demonstrate the actuality and fictiveness of the past. Our narrator is a dreamer and historian: "I have been searching for the entrance to the land of nonbeing in old maps endowed with ancient charm and wisdom. . . . There is only one place that is forever beyond the reach of our knowledge: the entrance to the land of the Peach Blossom Spring" (Peach Blossom

Spring is China's hidden paradise on earth that only a blessed traveler could chance upon).

He writes also of the political significance of maps and mapmakers: "There is no actually existing entity that serves as evidence of boundaries between districts or countries. Therefore, we can say that the boundary is a fictional exercise of power." Our final glimpse of the narrator in part 1 reveals him as a philosopher with aspirations to the divine:

> Unconsciously we have always yearned to be one with God. A map is no longer a utilitarian instrument but an epistemological translation of our knowledge of the world. The translated text will ultimately replace the limited vision of our individual selves, becoming a panoramic virtual space in our psyche and spirit, unfolding within our minds a total map that stretches into infinity. In this way we transcend ourselves and lose ourselves, for we are everywhere and nowhere.

Yet our narrator is never far from reality: "The ineffable bliss we experience [in reading maps] is similar to the effect produced by examining the floor plans of real estate sales brochures." Readers who stumbled in chapter 1 may in hindsight appreciate the changes of tone throughout part 1 that alternately baffle, inform, and amuse.

Part 2, "The City," introduces a more dramatic note, its first two chapters presenting an image of the city as a mirage. The narrative notes its disappearance and inquires into means of establishing its previous existence:

> The remaining maps of Victoria, which vary in quality but abound in quantity, are no guarantee of the city's

existence. On the contrary, they throw doubt on its stability and actuality. Reading them is like tracing a lover's inner topography. Under those oscillating, ambiguous, indefinite, and yet suggestive expressions, the map reader's knowledge and imagination are led into a meandering narrative, out of which is woven a novel full of prejudice, jealousy, misunderstanding, perplexity, anxiety, and ecstasy.

Some of part 2 is based on the memoirs of early governors describing their attempts to order Hong Kong's existence as a prosperous, well-governed city. A note records that "British cartography was first-class in the world in the nineteenth century, and many naval officers and colonial officials had advanced map-drawing skills." Other early visitors who left descriptions of early Hong Kong include a shipwrecked Japanese sailor, said to have been there in 1845. As the narrator comments, "Implausible passages in the text may be due to Kino's blurred memory or the result of the investigators' fertile imaginations."

The narrator recedes from personal intervention in part 2, but Barthes and Borges are present in name and in the narrator's thoughts:

A "plan" is a plane figure but also a design, a present visualization of future form. On the one hand it does not yet exist and is unreal, but on the other hand it is being designed and will be constructed. A plan is thus a kind of fiction, and the meaning of this fiction is inseparable from the design and blueprint.

Prompts such as these encourage readers to doubt the reality of these accounts. One of the most engaging is in chapter 24, on

Mr. Smith's one-day trip to the colony. Smith is an Englishman who visited Victoria for a day in August 1907. While his wife went to a hairdresser's (after several stormy days at sea), Smith took a stroll around town: mailing a letter home at the post office, buying books about Hong Kong in Kelly & Walsh, and buying seasickness medicine and whiskey from Watson & Co. The same shops are not necessarily in the same places, but the cityscape is recognizable; there appears to be no evidence for Mr. and Mrs. Smith's visit.

Even more curiously, chapter 25 contrasts the view from Government House as described by the tenth governor (1887–1891), Sir William Des Voeux, and its last (1992–1997), Chris Patten, the only difference being that the latter's words are not written but "alleged" remarks addressed by Patten to one of the gardeners. . . . At this point, almost halfway through the novel, even the most trusting reader is bound to start questioning every account appearing so far and throughout the rest of the book. Other bizarre events follow. In chapter 26, a monstrous toad rising from the harbor is seen in a dream and sketched by Captain Edward Belcher, although his sketch is lost.[2] The plague described in chapter 28 that caused thousands of deaths in the area around what is now Blake Garden was real, but not necessarily the parrots belonging to an English couple who perished, leaving the parrots to flourish in the giant banyan trees, or the investigators who more than a century later "suddenly hit upon the bright idea that generations of Blake Garden parrots might have passed down authentic vocalizations from the past. They went to Blake Garden with audio equipment to interview the birds' descendants, as if recording oral history."

A darker note is left to the last chapter. A military map of Victoria, designed by the British but with a Japanese text and frequently cited as evidence of Japan's ambitions in East Asia during World War II, is claimed by a Japanese historian to be no more than a war game popular in the middle of the twentieth century, not unlike the computer games that emerged toward the end of the century. In contrast, a Japanese novelist claims that an idle drawing he made as a child turned out many years later to be an accurate sketch of Victoria: "It was only in the 1960s that I learned that there was such a place as Victoria, and to my surprise the map of that city happened to coincide with the one that the lonely and introspective child had inadvertently made up in his utter boredom."

Published separately in translation, some of the chapters in part 3, "Streets," have been described as essays, but like the rest of the book, they form part of the author's fictional vision of Hong Kong. Each chapter gives a documented account of a street or neighborhood in Hong Kong—except that some, perhaps many, of the sources are imaginary. "Spring Garden Lane," for example, tells the story of a Mr. and Mrs. Parker, who are killed by bandits while walking in the hills above Happy Valley and whose son is then taken to England for his education; the son returns, marries into a local Chinese family, and spends the remainder of his life in Hong Kong. This biographical sketch is not obviously fictional, but the reader may conclude otherwise.

The narrator remains largely impersonal in part 3, recognizing folly in the foreigners' ways without being judgmental. In "Ice House Street" he relates how ice was imported for the benefit of the nineteenth-century colonists and concludes with a link to the current use of one of the street's old buildings as a venue for theater performances, serving the postcolonialists' cultural aspirations. The Cantonese confusion of "ice" with "snow" gives rise to a fantasy of a colonial ice cellar where nostalgic Englishmen and their wives suffering from the summer's heat would go underground to enjoy the ritual of afternoon tea in front of a fire.

Interaction between locals and colonialists outside of regulations can be fatal. In chapter 36, a government sanitation officer, forsaking the red-light district for foreigners in Lyndhurst Terrace, visits the Chinese brothels in Shui Hang Hau, where he falls madly in love with a local prostitute named Butterfly. When he dies in a fall one morning after spending the night with her, it is said that his demise was caused by his "possession" by the spirit of Butterfly's late father. Almost as ominous are the authorities' attempts to recover local traditions: as described in chapter 37, an area near Mong Kok known as Poetry, Song, and Dance that had degenerated under colonial rule into a red-light district was revived when the authorities replanted the street with bauhinia trees. Bauhinia is the city's emblematic flower, yet the tree is a sterile hybrid.

Chapter 38 relates administrative consternation with a street having one name in summer and another in winter: "If you sent a letter to Tung Choi Street in the summertime but wrote the name Sai Yeung Choi Street by mistake, it might be winter before it got delivered." The solution, to create two streets, only led to further muddle. Chapter 40 depicts an impossible geometry in a public square resembling an M. C. Escher painting, much studied by "the psychoanalytic school of cartography." The final chapter, "Cedar Street," performs a different kind of acrobatic feat by describing a book about maps by "a minor writer of the late twentieth century":

In this unsystematic and unclassifiable collection of map reading, and with a complete disregard for reality, the author read in between the dotted lines and colored spots strewn freely across the page all sorts of public and private nightmares, memories, longings, and speculations.

In part 4, "Signs," the narrator reconstructs twentieth-century Hong Kong through maps, blueprints, and humdrum relics of a lost civilization. It begins with "The Decline of the Legend" (the word "legend" remaining ambiguous):

> However, as legends developed, not only did they fail to expand the possibility of signs as a form of language; on the contrary, they turned into a limitation. To serve their instrumental purpose more efficiently, legends became uniform, compulsory supplements without any imaginative power to speak of. The language of maps became rigid. There was nothing in existence more arid than maps, which were reduced to games in the exercise of power, whether in regard to knowledge, economics, or politics. It is only when individual ways of reading legends return that we can again read legends as tales of marvels.

Among these tales of marvels is the difference between global economic and climatological readings of a map of 1985 and the study of "postgeology (representing the peak of agitation for indigenous cultural exploration)" at the University of Hong Kong. Science fiction has political undertones, such as the plan to evacuate Hong Kong by constructing a mobile "airport" at Chek Lap Kok "to cope with major catastrophes such as nuclear accidents, earthquakes, epidemics, or alien invasions." A group of tourists from the future explore a completely reconstructed city, shopping at Cat Street in Central for "replicas of heritage objects from the city's past: for example, broken plastic and metal toys, moldy faded martial arts novels with missing pages and pornographic magazines, nonfunctioning transistor radios, electric fans and typewriters, corroded copper kettles, tarnished silver ornaments, makeup cases made of rotten wood, out-of-date calendars, pocket watches that had stopped, and tattered and torn maps," returning to their hotel loaded with purchases. A transport timetable shows passengers on trains leaving the mainland border for the city as time travelers.

There is little overt challenge to the central Chinese government in *Atlas*, and there are writers all over China who are writing with similar affection about their own local histories. The difference in Dung Kai-cheung's case is that the colonial past is not demonized, and the play of his imagination is not confined by uneasy glances at the censor, whether linguistic, social, or political. This openness is subversive in a way that political censorship cannot control but that the authorities cannot support.

Dung Kai-cheung's *Atlas* and Calvino's *Invisible Cities* both consist of short chapters and combine urban fables with abstract fancies on the nature of the city. The differences are just as obvious: *Atlas* is free of orientalist imagery, for instance. In *Invisible Cities* one fantasy follows relentlessly after the other, and only the changing relationship between the power-obsessed emperor and the sex-obsessed traveler sustains the narrative interest; in *Atlas* the fantasies are extensions of the real and therefore endlessly intriguing. Whether or not Dung Kai-cheung consciously adopted *Invisible Cities* as a model, the comparison suggests that unfamiliar local references are not always a deterrent to nonlocal readers. The majority of Calvino's readers read *Invisible Cities* in translation, but neither his Italian-speaking nor his English-speaking readers would be familiar with the topography of Yuan-dynasty Peking. Localism, in this case, has not been a barrier to international appeal.

3

I have discussed at length elsewhere the difficulties that Hong Kong Chinese writers have found in reaching audiences outside Hong Kong, whether in Chinese in China or in translation abroad.[3]

One factor in the international inattention to Hong Kong literature by local writers may be Hong Kong's linguistic multiplicity. Most academic studies and journalistic reviews focus either on its English-language works or on its Chinese-language works, each appearing thinner without the other. There is also a widespread belief, going beyond cultural circles, that in regarding itself as the hub of Asia, Hong Kong is merely delusional: it is and only ever has been a border town, on the periphery of empire (British, Chinese) and not at anyone's center. The concept of "borrowed time, borrowed place," described and rejected by Dung Kai-cheung in his preface, may be another factor in the lack of attention outside East Asia given to Hong Kong writers and artists. It can of course be argued that Hong Kong still has an expiry date—it used to be 1997 but is now 2047, when its political and legal system is to give way to mainland rules. Hong Kong still has a giant next door: it is less threatening but also much more powerful than it used to be. Is Hong Kong a place with its own past and future, worthy of a literary culture created by its own people? Is its interest to the world outside no more than its exotic setting, or its frank commercial appeal as a place where anything can be bought and sold?

Hong Kong's population includes devoted readers: in contrast to Taiwan, bilingual bookshops are everywhere and packed with browsers, and the sixty-six branches of the Hong Kong Public Libraries are well stocked with titles in Chinese and English and well patronized. A city of six million Cantonese may lack the numbers to make publishing local fiction profitable (most of Dung Kai-cheung's novels have been published in Taipei), but there is a potential audience of Cantonese speakers in southern China larger than the audiences of native readers in several European countries. Nevertheless, Dung Kai-cheung's occasional use of

Cantonese expressions, his identity as a Hong Kong writer, and his preferred locality of Hong Kong discourage mainland readers preoccupied with the highlights and controversies at the center of China's elite culture.

Even setting aside language politics, why would anyone apart from Hong Kong Chinese want to read and study Hong Kong literature in Chinese? Is it worth translating, adapting or otherwise rewriting to bring to the attention of readers in the rest of China and the world? Must it be accepted in China before the rest of the world takes notice? Or is international recognition the prerequisite for gaining respect in China? In truth, none of the factors mentioned earlier (and none of these questions) may in the end count for much: a small handful of writers is sometimes enough to transform the image of small countries in the literary world. Dung Kai-cheung and his fellow writers are just now part of that transformation.

The new awareness of Hong Kong history as a source for Cantonese fiction can be dated to around 1984 with the appearance of *Yanzhi kou (Rouge)*, by Lee Bik-Wah (also known as Li Bihua and Lillian or Lilian Lee). Lee's novel, which has not been translated into English, is available in all Hong Kong bookstores, and the film of the same name (1988) is also a longtime Hong Kong favorite. The main narrative of the novel is in Mandarin, although parts of the dialogue are in Cantonese. Together with its strong sense of place, its street names, building names, and so on, the novel targets a local audience. *Rouge* contrasts Hong Kong in the present (1980) and fifty years earlier (in the 1930s), linked by the ghost whose hopeless love is the basis of the plot. Written at the time of negotiations on retrocession, it resurrects a Hong Kong past that is neither British nor mainland but uniquely Hong Kong, and it has contributed to the development of local pride in the territory's historical relics.

It is fitting that a ghost is responsible for this awakening sense of the past, since much of that past was already destroyed and can live on, ghostlike, only in museums or in the loving re-creations of the film studios.

Eileen Chang's much earlier *Qing cheng zhi lian* (*Love That Topples a City*; translated as *Love in a Fallen City*) (1943) has met a similar fate.[4] The location is again central to the plot: Hong Kong is a place where personal dreams of liberation as well as wealth can be realized by its Shanghai immigrants. When the film version of *Love in a Fallen City* appeared in 1985, the Hong Kong audience was enraptured once again: the nostalgic re-creation of historical sites then already reduced to rubble, the décor, costumes, and hotel settings, all appealed to the audience's expectations and memories. Outside Hong Kong (and fans of Hong Kong), the film, like the novel itself, made little impact.

The nostalgia of the 1980s persists but is accompanied by more robust contributions. Xi Xi and Wong Bik Wan (writing in Chinese) and Xu Xi (writing in English) in present-day Hong Kong fiction, and Louise Ho (writing in English) and Leung Ping-kwan, Wong Kwok-pun, and Ng Mei-kwan (writing in Chinese) in poetry are among many writers highly regarded in local literary circles but hardly known beyond them. To many readers and critics, *Atlas* not only is one of the most captivating works to come out of Hong Kong in recent years but also points to the maturity of Hong Kong in the world of letters. Quite apart from its conspicuous wealth, urban excitements, and tranquil countryside, Hong Kong has a strong claim on the attention of readers in China and in the rest of the world. Given that censorship of literary works in Hong Kong is virtually nonexistent, Hong Kong literature provides documentation from the margins on the values of diversity, individual autonomy, and imaginative freedom.

4

My first acquaintance with Dung Kai-cheung's work came through translating chapters of *Atlas* for undergraduate classes in literary translation at the Chinese University of Hong Kong in 2006 and 2007. The students were a mixed group of Hong Kong residents and mainlanders who had come to Hong Kong for university studies. The local students were keen to include Hong Kong literary texts in the course, and the mainlanders were willing to agree, so the final selection included poetry by Leung Ping-kwan and fiction by Dung Kai-cheung as well as mainland writing. The chapters from part 3 of *Atlas* raised challenging translation issues and were also of suitable length and level of difficulty for class translation. First "Spring Garden Lane" and the following year "Ice House Street" were great hits for the students and teacher alike. All of us owe much to Wong Nim-yan, who first recommended *Atlas* to me and then patiently explained the meanings, the background, and the fantasies: for this and very much more I am deeply grateful.

The final version of "Spring Garden Lane" by Wong Nim-yan and me was eventually published in the Hong Kong journal *Renditions*, a magazine for translations of Chinese literature into English. A delay was caused by the journal's policy of romanizing all Chinese words and proper nouns in the Hanyu Pinyin system (the PRC's replacement for foreign-based romanization for standard northern Chinese, such as Wade-Giles in English-language works). This policy had its origins in the journal's mission when it was founded in 1973 during China's Cultural Revolution but was not appropriate for works written in Cantonese about Hong Kong, and it was changed under the editorship of Anders Hansson from 2006 to 2008. "Spring Garden Lane" duly appeared in 2006 with its Cantonese words and names in Cantonese romanization.

It was during this drawn-out process that Anders Hansson and I became acquainted with Dung Kai-cheung and drew up plans to translate *Atlas*. Each of us took responsibility for one or two parts, and each of us read and checked each other's drafts. It took about two years, partly because of the density of the writing, in particular the complex intertwining of fiction, fact, and theory (or antitheory). It culminated in a four-hour meeting in a café in a Sha Tin mall where we debated the final harmonization of names of people, places, and even a Spanish ship. It was at this meeting that Dung Kai-cheung decided to alter his Chinese text to accommodate some of the questions raised in the translation. I think each of us found the process exhausting, but for Anders Hansson and me, it was also a revelation of aspects of Hong Kong that we'd not previously encountered.

Our common goal all along was to reach a general readership, not just students and academics in Chinese studies. With this in mind, we chose not to give notes (apart from those in the original text) or to rewrite our working glossary into a formal index. The pleasure of this work lies in its literary imagination and historical reflections, qualities we hope will appeal to all of its readers.

Bonnie S. McDougall
Donnini
June 2011

NOTES

This introduction was written while I was a fellow of the Santa Maddalena Foundation. I am most grateful to the director, Beatrice Monti della Corte, her assistants Ted Hodgkinson and Emma Hamilton, and fellow writers Terry Tempest Williams, Kamila Shamsie, and Javier Montes for their generosity and warmth.

1. First published in 1972; English translation 1978. If comparisons must be drawn, then W. G. Sebald's *Die Ausgewanderten* (1992; published in English translation as *The Emigrants*, 1996) is closer although not named in the novel itself.

2. Belcher compiled the 1841 "Hong Kong Nautical Chart," the first scientific survey map with Hong Kong Island as its object and also the first map of Hong Kong under British rule.

3. "Diversity as Value: Marginality, Post-colonialism and Identity in Modern Chinese Literature," in *Belief, History and the Individual in Modern Chinese Literary Culture*, ed. Artur K. Wardega (Newcastle upon Tyne: Cambridge Scholars, 2009), 137–65.

4. Translated by Karen Kingsbury in *Renditions* 45 (spring 1996): 61–92.

PART ONE

Theory

COUNTERPLACE

"Macao Roads," drawn in 1810, demonstrated for the first time the possibility of a theory of counterplace. According to an ancient and almost forgotten saying, every place that appears on a map must have one or more counterplaces. This knowledge had been invalidated in the development of scientific mapmaking, and it regained attention only recently through extended researches into ancient maps.

"Macao Roads" was jointly produced by Daniel Ross and Philip Maughan, lieutenants of the Bombay Marine, for the British East India Company. At its center are the waters around what was later known as Hong Kong (including Hong Kong Island, the Kowloon Peninsula, the New Territories, and the Outlying Islands), while Macao only appears at the far left (west) of the map.

Placed in the middle of "Macao Roads" is an island named Hung Kong (literally, "red river"), and to its southeast lies a bay called Tytam (big load). To the north of Hung Kong, across a natural harbor, is a peninsula attached to the mainland. A place called Cowloon (nine lanes) lies to the northeast of the peninsula. East of the harbor dividing Hung Kong from the mainland are two entrances, called Ly-ee-moon (gate of ceremonial garments) and Fo-tow-moon (gate of the fiery head), respectively, while the entrance to the northwest of the harbor is called Cap-sing-moon (gate of quick thought). Southwest of Hung Kong lies an island called Lama (blue hemp), and to its west lies another island called Tyho (big inlet) or Lantao, which has an area three times bigger than Hung Kong. A bay called Ty-po-hoy (big cloth opening) is located in the northeast of the mainland.

If we compare this map to other maps with similar topographic characteristics produced around the same time, we will discover numerous corresponding pairs in the local pronunciation, like Red River and Incense Harbor (also known as Fragrant Harbor), Big Load and Big Pool, Nine Lanes and Nine Dragons, Gate of Ceremonial Garments and Gate of Carps, Gate of the Fiery Head and Gate of the Buddhist Hall, Gate of Quick Thought and Gate of Pumping Water, Blue Hemp and Southern Fork, Big Inlet and Big Oyster, and finally Big Cloth Opening and Big Land Sea. This is evidence that, in the mimetic world of maps, a place will inevitably find its counterplace in another, parallel space. A Platonic relationship exists between counterplaces, that is, both (or more) are copies or simulacra of a common "reality" or "idea." Or, to put it in other words, both are translations of an "original text." The mutual reliance of counterplaces is built on their common connection with the same origin. Yet this connection only points at another name. The name "Hong Kong" allows both Red River and Fragrant Harbor to become distinct but not mutually exclusive "really existing" places.

Going further, Hung Kong (empty harbor), Tai Dam (big mouthful), Kow Lung (leaning on), Lai Yee Mun (gate of the little rascal), Fai Dau Mun (gate of the quick knife), Kap See Mun (gate of timeliness), Lan Ma (blocking the horse), Lan Tau (broken head), and Tai Bo Hoi (taking big strides) all become possible names (and as such possible places) on the "Macao Roads" of my memories and longings.

2

COMMONPLACE

When we study ancient maps, we find repeatedly that places with the same name appear in different forms. These places lumped together under one name are not in fact the same place but common places. Although they are not the same place, they have something in common. This is how the term "commonplace" is defined.

Examples of commonplaces are numerous. Take, for example, a place called Hung Heung Lou Shan (literally, "red incense burner mountain"). There is a small island called Hung Heung Lou shown on a map of San-on County (an area roughly corresponding to the Pearl River Delta) in the 1819 edition of the *San-on County Gazetteer*. Here the island is situated at the near southwest of the Kowloon Peninsula, to the north of Yeung Suen Chau and Kap Shui Mun. In an anonymous map drawn before 1840, entitled "A Map of the China Coast," however, Hung Heung Lou Shan has been moved to the south of Yeung Suen Chau and its distance from Kowloon increased fivefold. This island is long and narrow, lying crosswise from the northwest to the southeast. Another "Map of San-on County" in the 1864 edition of the *Guangdong Provincial Gazetteer* shows a regularly shaped island called Hung Heung Lou Shun smack in the middle of waters south of Kowloon.

Given the similarities in their names and their overall relationship with landmarks in the general vicinity, it is safe to conclude that Hung Heung Lou, Hung Heung Lou Shan, and Hung Heung Lou Shun are commonplaces. Nevertheless, we must be on our guard against taking it for granted that they are the same place, for no place on any map can ever be the same place as any other place on any other map. Every map has its own set of places, and every place belongs exclusively to its own map. Therefore, no one single place could ever transgress the map to which it owes its existence and become one with another place. If similar configurations appear on different maps, it is because of the fact that these places are commonplaces to one another. The Red Incense Burner of 1819, 1840, and 1864 cannot be the same Red Incense Burner, but each of them can only be the Red Incense Burner of the maps labeled "1819," "1840," and "1864," respectively.

As a matter of fact, these Red Incense Burners are commonplaces to the place called Hong Kong at a later age (or in another time and space), so that we come to the conclusion that Hong Kong is also a commonplace. It follows that when every place has its commonplaces, each of these places loses its distinctive character and becomes simply a common place. No place can transcend itself to attain an eternal and absolute state. When each and every place reiterates its existence through common means, replicating one another's commonality and vainly attempting to raise this commonality to the highest degree, its repetitive self-affirmation may end up as a stale convention. This is the reason that modern maps of high precision lack imagination.

By making people forget that places can relate to one another only as commonplaces, these conventions fool us into believing that any place has always been the same—forever fixed and immutable.

MISPLACE

In the map in the 1819 edition of the *San-on County Gazetteer*, Tuen Mun Shun (garrison gate high water) is situated among a group of islands in the sea to the west of Kowloon Shun, standing next to Pui To Shan (cup crossing mountain). On the "Map of San-on County" in the 1864 edition of the *Guangdong Provincial Gazetteer*, however, Tuen Mun O (garrison gate bay) appears among the mountains on the eastern side of the mainland, to the north of Ma On Shan (saddle mountain), facing Pui To Shan from afar. Further, if we consult the 1897 edition of the *Guangdong Provincial Gazetteer*, we discover that Tuen Mun Shun has been relocated to the western side of the mainland, inside a bay called Tuen Mun (regiment gate), written with a different character for Tuen.

There are two questions that concern us here: first, the misrepresentation of the location of the place signified as Tuen Mun; second, the misrepresentation of certain locations on the maps as Tuen Mun. These two points imply that a misplaced place will always deprive another place of its correct representation, resulting in a double misreading. That is to say that, first of all, Tuen Mun is not where it "should be," and second that Tuen Mun occupies a place where it "should not be." Therefore, the prefix "mis" in "misplace" carries both the meaning of "wrongly taking one thing as another one" as in "mistake" or "misunderstand," and the meaning of "should not be" as in "misbehavior." As for the concept of "place," in this school of thought, it can be understood as "representation" from the perspective of production, or as "reading" from the perspective of reception. In fact, "representation" and "reading" are just two sides of the same coin.

We can, for convenience's sake, call this school cartocentric, since its members do not believe in any objective reality outside maps. Cartocentric scholars are totally unconcerned about the correct location of Tuen Mun and even deny the legitimacy of such questions. Their investigation is wholly preoccupied in how the "place" called Tuen Mun is being represented and read. According to this view, all representations of places are simultaneously both right and wrong: in whatever place Tuen Mun appears, it cannot be invalidated by factors exterior to the map. By the same token, anywhere that Tuen Mun appears is destined to be wrong. From this is derived the thesis that "all places are misplaces, and all misplaces are misreadings." The map is regarded as the only operational field of spatial senses.

Investigations from this angle suggest that Hong Kong is also a misplace. Its appearance and evolution in the history of cartography inevitably imply meanings of mistakes, misunderstanding, and misdoing. However, it is also owing to this very inevitability and actuality that it earns legitimacy and correctness, at least literally so.

It is evident that the passion of the cartocentrics in rejecting and rebutting empirical knowledge does not necessarily elevate them above other schools of thought. It remains but one of many competing theories, all perhaps motivated by the desire to control the object of knowledge by seizing the ultimate power of interpretation.

Scholars, in truth, are no different from suspicious and possessive lovers whose derangement only increases the more deeply they probe, since lovers always fix their eyes on misplaces.

4

DISPLACE

The term "displace" can be understood in a narrow and a broad sense. In the narrow sense, it means that the position of one place is taken over by another place in the diachronic development of mapmaking. A good example can be found in "A Coastal Map of Guangdong" in *A Comprehensive Account of Guangdong Province*, written by Guo Fei in the late sixteenth century. This map is oriented in such a way that it faces toward the South China Sea from the mainland with the south at the top. It shows a big island across the water to the south of the Kwun Foo Guard Post (Kowloon Hills), on which Chek Chue occupies the center and is surrounded by places named Wong Nai Chung, Tai Tam, and Shau Kei Wan. To the southwest from the big island (by its upper right on the map), a small, lonely island named Hong Kong stands in the sea. Comparing "A Coastal Map of Guangdong" with some later maps, however, we discover that the location of the big island opposite Kowloon is taken over by Hong Kong or Hung Heung Lou. In the 1819 edition of the *San-on County Gazetteer*, Chek Chue has clearly been pushed farther south into the sea by Hung Heung Lou, becoming itself a small, isolated island. In "A Map of the Waterways of Guangdong Province" produced by a magistrate by the name of Chen in 1840, Chek Chue returns for the last time to a central position in the harbor. Nevertheless, Chek Chue is again displaced by Hung

Heung Lou Shun in "A Map of San-on County" in the *Guangdong Provincial Gazetteer* of 1864, and it even disappears from the map.

It can be said that in this process of transformation, Chek Chue was gradually displaced by Hung Heung Lou, and Hung Heung Lou was displaced in turn by Hong Kong. There are two ways in which this displacement could have taken place. The first is Hong Kong (or Hung Heung Lou) displacing the place Chek Chue. This is a form of geographical transfer (at least geographical as understood in the context of cartographical discourse). In the second way, the signifier "Hong Kong" displaced the signifier "Chek Chue" and became the name of a more or less specific place on the map. No matter which is the case, it implies that one place can be replaced by another at any time, and the place being taken over will never be the same as before even though its form and position may remain unchanged.

There exists an even more radical theory that attempts to define the concept of "displace" in a broad sense, and in so doing extends it to a general and fundamental level. According to this theory, every place on a map is a displace. A place is never itself but is forever displaced by another. This is also to say that the map itself is a displacement, and cartography is such a process of displacement. No matter whether we understand them from the perspective of teleology or of utilitarianism, and no matter how scientifically and with what exactitude they are produced, maps have never been copies of the real world but are displacements. In the end, the real world is totally supplanted in the process of displacement and fades from human cognition. The sight of the Guangdong coast in the sixteenth century is forever beyond reach, but not the sight of the sixteenth century "Coastal Map of Guangdong."

Traditional cartography seemingly instructs us on how to recognize and search for places, but in fact its real lesson is that we can never arrive at our desired place on the map, and yet, at the same time, we inevitably arrive at its displace.

5

ANTIPLACE

The "Map of the Sun-on-district," drawn by the Italian missionary Simeone Volonteri in 1866, delineates in minute detail the positions of villages on the British-governed Hong Kong Island and Kowloon Peninsula as well as in the adjacent areas of San-on County, which at the time was still Chinese territory. Father Volonteri's original plan was to have the map engraved in London, so as to acquire enough subscribers to cover the expenses of publication, and with the map would be attached a free copy of a pamphlet on cartography written by Volonteri himself. The engraving was eventually done in Leipzig for considerations of cost, while the complimentary pamphlets were discontinued following complications in matters of distribution. It is said, however, that two hundred copies of the pamphlets had been printed in London, although with the exception of a few copies presented as gifts to fellow cartographers, none survived the passage of time.

In his pamphlet, Volonteri proposed the concept of antiplace and illustrated it with examples from his "Map of the Sun-on-district." It might be conjectured that the "Map of the Sun-on-district" was in fact a supplement for the purpose of illustrating the concept of antiplace. Since the pamphlets were lost while the maps survived, the theory of antiplace also fell into oblivion. It is now impossible to reconstruct Volonteri's theory of antiplace. The most anyone can do is to piece together fragments of information scattered among surviving sources.

When the conditions of two places are the diametrical opposites of each other, Volonteri calls them antiplaces. The establishment of antiplaces has nothing to do with the relative positions of two places on a map. Any two points at the ends of any diameter of the earth, thus opposite each other in position on the surface of the sphere, are called antipodes. An example of antipodes is the North Pole and the South Pole, but since they have virtually no difference in weather conditions and environment, that is, in their state of being, they cannot be regarded as antiplaces. The methods of searching for or calculating antiplaces are no longer known to the modern cartographer, and the only example left is to be found in Volonteri's "Map of the Sun-on-district."

In the "Map of the Sun-on-district," there is a place on the Kowloon Peninsula called Mong Kok (mango point), which is said to be the antiplace of Sha Tau Kok (sand head point), on the coast of the northeastern mainland on the map. By 1866, the Kowloon Peninsula was British territory, while Sha Tau Kok was still under the rule of the Qing dynasty. It was not until 1898 that Sha Tau Kok, as an insignificant part of the newly leased New Territories, came under British rule. After that, Sha Tau Kok became a guard post on the Sino-British boundary. According to the antiplace theory, Mong Kok and Sha Tau Kok represent, respectively, the center and the periphery of Hong Kong, each related to the other as polar opposites. In the twentieth century, Mong Kok became a commercial district with the highest population density in the territory, while the name Sha Tau Kok has become a synonym for "wilderness" in colloquial usage, with connotations of backwardness and dereliction. This is the interpretation offered by scholars who have studied Volonteri's postulation of Mong Kok and Sha Tau Kok as antiplaces, but the question of how Volonteri could, in 1866, predict what was going to happen to the two places in the century ahead is still short of a satisfactory answer.[1]

There is another argument to the effect that the "anti" in "antiplace" originates from the word "antithesis," such that "antiplace" means "antithetical place." The term "antithesis" should here be understood in its rhetorical sense, that is, the pairing of opposite ideas in speech or writing for apologetic effects. The opposition of Mong Kok and Sha Tau Kok generates a series of rhetorical antitheses, for example segregation/integration, distance/proximity, separation/reunion, oblivion/remembrance, hate/love. This is why one can say that antiplace *is* antithesis, and place *is* thesis. Mong Kok and Sha Tau Kok can be characterized as being in a relationship that has love as its thesis.

This actually coincides with a third interpretation of the term "antiplace." In this theory "anti" is explained as "going against" or "undoing," so that being an antiplace means to desert, betray, subvert, forget, and deny the physicality of a place and to deprive it of its material existence, and in so doing turning it into something abstract: a concept, name, image, impression, desire, or fantasy. The meaning of a place for us is thus no longer general, objective, and scientific but individual and irrational—a kind of irrational thesis.

[1] For further studies on the "Map of the Sun-on-district," see the *Geographical Journal*, June 1969, and the *Journal of the Royal Asiatic Society*, 1970.

NONPLACE

Nonplace does not mean no place, nor does it mean a nonexistent place. It just lacks certain conditions that a place should have, such as a name and a referential reality. Commonsense tells us that to have a name but no referential reality, or to have referential reality but no name, does not count as a "place" in the strict sense. Yet, for a cartographer, so long as it is included in the area of a map, even though it does not have a name or a referential reality, no two-dimensional space at any bearing should ever be denied the legitimacy of being a "place." It is for this reason that we call this kind of "place" to which attaches no name and no referential reality a "nonplace."

Two nonplaces appear on the map of the 1819 edition of the *San-on County Gazetteer*. One of them appears in the waters south of Kowloon Shun, as an island surrounded by Yeung Suen Chau, Chek Chue, Po Toi, Fook Kin Tau, and Tai Kam Mun. The rectangular label above the image of the island is left blank, unlike other, similar rectangles, which have names. To the west of Kowloon Shun and to the north of Lei Yu Mun Fortress and Tuen Mun Shun, another blank label lies over the waters. Again, a large unnamed island, which appears to the east of Lantao in "A Sketch of the Islands to the S.E. of Lantao on the Coast of China," drawn by Chinese hands and printed by Alexander Dalrymple in 1786, may well be another case of nonplace. There are also records of nonplaces on maps drawn by foreigners, a good example being Captain Hayter's 1780 "A Chart of the China Sea from the Island of Sanciam to Pedra Branca." A relatively small, obscure island to the east of a larger island called He-ong-kong would also seem to fall into the category of nonplace.

Cartographers have disputed for years the causes of nonplaces and their significance. Some say that nonplaces appear to satisfy people's fantasies about unknown places; others propose the opposite, claiming that the existence of nonplaces actually negates our knowledge of places, for a nonplace is a place that does not exist, a mirror image, a mirage that is visible but intangible, and that exists but is not to be experienced.

Later scholars have established that the nonplace of Dalrymple's "A Sketch of the Islands to the S.E. of Lantao on the Coast of China" in 1786 is actually what eventually became known as Hong Kong Island.

7

EXTRATERRITORIALITY

Extraterritoriality has always been a controversial concept in cartographical studies. The term "territory" has never been a simple and neutral indication of a place but implies by necessity occupation, subordination, and administration, all of which carry connotations of a master-servant power relation. It demonstrates how an authority legitimizes its possession of a place, and how this process of legitimization is inevitably implemented through the production of maps. This argument alone is enough to disprove the attempts of some scholars at delimiting cartography as merely a set of technical exercises based on natural geographical realities. For maps are not just a depiction, record, or symbol of power but the actual execution of power itself. The scramble for territorial sovereignty over places through acts of documentation has always been an alternative battlefield, apart from direct warfare, between countries and between power entities.

The concept of extraterritoriality is hardly imaginable given the boundless desire of powers to territorize places, and it is incompatible with the nature of mapmaking as a means of territorization. Yet we do not have much difficulty in finding examples of extraterritoriality in the literature of cartography. In a German map from 1834 called "The Chinese Coast of the Province of Kwang-tung on Both Sides of the Meridian of Macao," we can see that along the green coastline there are two islands marked in red called Hong Kong and Lamma. According to the explanation on the map, this map is based on "Macao Roads," the marine chart drawn by Ross and Maughan in 1810. The later map is improved in accuracy, but the fact that Hong Kong Island and Lamma Island are printed in red remains puzzling. It is said that the general practice in those days was to represent British territory in red. However, Hong Kong had not yet become a British colony in the year the map was produced. Does this imply that Hong Kong had already ceased to be a part of Chinese territory in the year 1834 and had become an extraterritory that was independent of, or rather abandoned by, the rest of the world?

An extraterritory can be indicated by markings dissimilar from those for ordinary territories, but it can also be done in the opposite manner. In the map "The Coast of South China" drawn in China about 1850 by an unknown person, we can see that to the south of Kwun Foo Shan, Kowloon Fort, and Yeung Suen Chau there remains only empty waters where Hong Kong Island should have lain. It seems that the method of exclusion has been employed to render invisible the fact of Hong Kong's being a part of Chinese territory. In fact, Hong Kong had already been ceded to the British by that time. The subtle thing about the map is that, while excluding Hong Kong from Chinese territory, it denies the possession of Hong Kong by the British at the same time. By wiping British Hong Kong off the map, it banishes Hong Kong to the realm of extraterritoriality. The act signifies a refusal to accept any sovereign authority or even a complete repudiation of the existence of sovereignty itself, for an extraterritory is a place that cannot be possessed or territorized. It exists forever outside omnipresent power, which is also to say that it does not exist. Only places that do not exist can escape being possessed.

More radical scholars of cartography point out that extraterritoriality means a quality of being rather than an actual place. As such, any place can have extraterritoriality and can possibly become an extraterritory. The question is, is this extraterritoriality intrinsic to the place or is it imparted extrinsically through some methods of depiction? This controversy has been heatedly debated but remains unresolved, with both sides demonstrating equal strength in argument and eloquence. Those who hold the former view are dreamers of an idyllic world, who oppose human civilization and an anthropocentric culture of power; they fantasize that land could be only land and nothing more, and that the world should be left to living creatures. In contrast, the latter are cartocentric nihilists who believe in maps as the only reality, outside of which nothing exists. For them, everything on maps essentially acquires a kind of extraterritoreality. Through this interpretation, they challenge the power of territorialization, for in the irrevocable passage of time, maps are no longer tools of defining, depicting, and constructing territories, rather they have taken the place of territories themselves, in a mockery of the futility of the exertion of power. Different paths lead to the same goal.

BOUNDARY

If we take a careful look at the map for the lease of Kowloon (before it was formally ceded) that was attached to the Treaty of Tientsin in 1860, one or two thought-provoking points will naturally catch our attention regarding the straight line cutting across the northern part of the Kowloon Peninsula from east to west. In the east the line begins at Kowloon Fort, and in the west it ends at the northern point of Yeung Suen Chau (later called Ong Suen Chau, or "tossing boat island"). San-on County lies north of the line and to the south is the Kowloon Peninsula. Near the line are the words "This area is hilly wasteland." If we suppose that maps are flat simulations of real places, then it follows that the really existing place, whether before or after the line was drawn, was basically unaffected. The hilly wasteland remained a hilly wasteland at the place where the straight line crosses it. This kind of line, which we name a boundary, is essentially different from other linear representations (for example, of coastlines or river systems) in mapmaking. In the eyes of traditional, science-oriented cartographers, the drawings of landforms always have their referents in reality, while boundaries exist only on maps. There is no actually existing entity that serves as evidence of boundaries between districts or countries.

Therefore, we can say that the boundary is a fictional exercise of power.

We may ask, how do we know whether we have transgressed the boundary on a wide stretch of hilly wasteland without partitions or labels? How do we experience the feeling of crossing the boundary? How do we prevent transgression? Or how do we construct the crime of transgression? An invisible boundary is more powerful and ruthless than a natural geographical barrier in forcing a dissection of nondifferentiated space. Thus, when you stand on the north side of the boundary, you are inside San-on County and outside British Kowloon. But take a step forward and you will be inside British Kowloon and outside San-on County. To be inside a place means at the same time that you are outside other places, and vice versa. In other words, all outsides are a form of being inside and all insides are a form of being outside. There is no absolute inside, nor is there an absolute outside. From this perspective, the fixing of boundaries is a way of making a place a place. Since there is no place on earth that has an absolute existence, all places (or all human understanding of places) are areas within boundaries, and power interprets areas as territories with boundaries.

A boundary is not just not an imitation of the real world, it is actually a fictional molding of the real world. In the formulation and implementation of the boundary, the world copies the map. Objects like stones or fences that mark the boundary in the real world do not appear prior to the drawing of the line on the map, and maps are certainly not records of the prior existence of these objects. On the contrary, such labeling objects are imitations of the imaginary line on the map. Therefore, the boundary between Kowloon and San-on County exists in the first place on the map, and the world is transformed according to the blueprint. An excellent example of the world imitating a map is Boundary Street.[2]

The prerequisite for the setting of boundaries on maps is possession of the power to create fiction.

[2] Boundary Street was a major street across the northern part of the Kowloon Peninsula. It was originally the boundary between British and Chinese territory as stipulated in the Convention of Beijing of 1860. However, a road was constructed along the boundary in the early twentieth century after the New Territories had been leased to the British and the boundary moved much farther north.

2

UTOPIA

If we open a traditional textbook on cartography and look up the section on map reading, we will find the following explanation: "Topographical map reading, or topographical map interpretation, is a method of gaining knowledge about the objective geographical environment through topographical maps. The process of map reading involves the reader recognizing signs on maps, thereby making the information received interact with the original spatial images registered by the cognitive faculties of the cerebrum, and in so doing transforming the reading of signs into knowledge of the geographical environment."

However, for a map reader like you or me, the ultimate aim of reading a map is no longer knowledge of the actual geographical environment. With the increase in knowledge of the geographical environment held by human civilization, there is no longer any place on the surface of the earth left unknown, so that the sense of amazement and exultation in discovering virgin lands in the great age of navigation is a blessing that our age is forever denied. Our age is crammed with so much knowledge that no space for the imagination is left. In the foreseeable future, the totality of all scientifically produced maps will allow us to know all knowable land on the surface of the earth. There is only one place that is forever beyond the reach of our knowledge: the entrance to the land of the Peach Blossom Spring.

Therefore, we forlorn beings of the contemporary world have no choice but to set out on a search for this land of nonbeing. Yet we no longer hold out hope of finding it in forests or valleys, or on wasteland or desert islands, nor do we have faith in the ability of airplanes, ships, cars, or even our own legs to take us to this undiscovered spot. Only on a map can we find a land that has never been trodden and never will be. For a map reader with an adventurous spirit, reading a map amounts to the art of navigation. Amid thunder and lightning, surging waves and torrential downpours, and tempests that disturb magnetic fields and distort compasses, the map reader dreams of a brave new world a thousand leagues in the depths of the sea.

Such people are mocked by orthodox cartographers as utopian map readers, or utopian mad readers. As a self-professed scholar of cartography who has also joined the ranks of these map readers, I am always beset by contradictory and confused feelings. Can academic research also be subjective, or even consist of imaginative projections and speculations? Can there be a kind of personal scholarship, as Roland Barthes proposes in *Camera Lucida*: a utopian "impossible science of the unique being"?

I have been searching for the entrance to the land of nonbeing in old maps endowed with ancient charm and wisdom. If maps can harbor secrets, I'd imagined that they would have to be excavated from fragmented, moth-eaten documents rather than from so-called scientifically rendered modern charts. In the course of these cartographic ramblings, mistakenly regarded by others (and even myself) as academic research, I stopped at various names, just as boats seek moorings in harbors. In maps, names usually have more referential power than symbols. We cannot imagine how a map with no names could refer to an actually existing place; names are the only guarantee of referentiality. However, names frequently possess the greatest imaginative ambiguity. They conjure up a series of landscapes in front of your eyes more vivid than can be drawn by contour lines or use of colors for different kinds of vegetation. Eventually I came to understand that the entrance was not to be found in the hidden depths of forests nor in the boundless expanse of deserts, but in names.

Two names brought me to the land of nonbeing. The first is Chun Fa Lok (spring flowers falling), which appears on "A Coastal Map of Guangdong" in *A Comprehensive Account of Guangdong Province*, drawn by Guo Fei in the late sixteenth century. This map adopts a panoramic perspective from the land to the sea and from north to south and has a small island named Chun Fa Lok in the waters facing Kwai Chung (sunflower waterway) and Tsin Wan (shallow bay). As a name for an island, Chun Fa Lok could hardly be more entrancing. When its spring flowers wither and fall, they would form a vista as of a land covered with red azalea. What kind of a place could it be where flowers fall all year round? Would it be a memory of a magnificent spring, or a lament for the withered flowers that follow? Compared with the Peach Blossom Spring, it would be less bustling and more desolate, less hopeful and more elegiac. Chun Fa Lok is a fallen Peach Blossom Spring, a soft-lens version of paradise lost. But it isn't without a faint trace of joy and promise, for when petals fall and berries ripen, summer will be a time of fruitfulness. A land of ever-falling spring flowers is a place that has never existed.

The second name is Fanchin Chow, which appears as the name of an island in "A Chart of Part of the Coast of China, and the Adjacent Islands from Pedro Blanco to the Mizen," drawn by Alexander Dalrymple, Scottish geographer and first hydrographer to the British Admiralty, in the years 1760 to 1770. The topological features of several places on this marine chart remain uncertain, while the coastline of the mainland and islands is also incomplete, leaving many blank spaces open to speculation, and place-names are given only in romanized form, without Chinese characters. What could "Fanchin Chow" refer to? What was it originally called in Chinese? Is it possible that it does not have a Chinese name? Could it mean "boating in a shallow craft" (*fan tsin chao*)? Isn't boating in a shallow craft an action associated with the Peach Blossom Spring? I seem to have ventured deep into the source of a mystical waterway aboard this shallow craft, arriving at the land of nonbeing, secluded from the human world.

The land is called nonbeing because it does not exist. All it is exists only as a name on the map.

According to later researchers, Chun Fa Lok is the place subsequently known as Tsing Yi (green garment) Island, while Fanchin Chow is Hong Kong Island. But these findings are beside the point for a map reader like me.

10

SUPERTOPIA

Borges tells us the story about a map that becomes one with the empire.

In his essay "On the Impossibility of Drawing a Map of the Empire on a Scale of 1 to 1,"[3] Umberto Eco proposes three hypotheses on how to make such a "total map" and then proceeds to disprove the viability of these methods. The three methods are as follows: first, to extend in midair a half-transparent sheet of a size equal to the empire, and then mark from above point by point on the sheet the corresponding topography below; second, to hang above the empire a nontransparent sheet of equal size, and then project the geographical details vertically upward from below; third, to cover the empire with a transparent, foldable, and adjustable sheet of air- and water-permeable material, so that all points on the map fully coincide with the land they represent. In actual practice, all three methods have in themselves insurmountable technical difficulties and irresolvable logical contradictions. (For details please see Eco's essay.)

---

[3] Umberto Eco, "On the Impossibility of Drawing a Map of the Empire on a Scale of 1 to 1," in *How to Travel with a Salmon and Other Essays*, trans. William Weaver (Orlando: Harcourt Brace, 1995).

The major problem lies not in technical considerations but in the very concept of a one-to-one total map. Eco points out correctly the paradox involved: when a total map is placed, in whatever way, on the surface of the empire, the material existence of the map itself has already become an inseparable part of the topography of the empire. Therefore, if the map is to be a faithful copy of the total geographical configuration of the empire, it has to include itself in its representation, that is, to demonstrate its own state of being placed on the surface of the empire. In order to reflect accurately and faithfully the fact of the map's being placed on the surface of the empire, it necessitates the erection of another map over against the former one. It follows logically that in order for the hypothesis of the one-to-one total map to stand, there needs to be an infinite overlaying of maps. The proposition is clearly untenable.

The futility of Eco's brilliant mind game lies in his unnecessary hypothesis that a map can faithfully reproduce every single detail on the surface of the earth, including its inhabitants, that is to say, the actual condition of those who constitute the producers and users of the map. In fact, the nature of a map is not to imitate and its ultimate goal not to become equivalent to the earth. On the contrary, its inner drive is to master the earth, or to mold the earth, or even to substitute itself for the earth as the field of real human interactions. The earth itself has become the pretext for such interactions. The scientific methods and mathematical calculations in the production of maps (i.e., control of bearings, elevation, and scale; methods of projection for the highest accuracy in perspective, area, and distance) ultimately do not serve the purpose of reflecting reality but proclaim the rights of ownership, exploitation, and interpretation of the earth.

Therefore, all places on maps are supertopias, places that supersede other places and are positioned over the earth, and as such they are more orderly than the earth and subject to more convenient manipulation, modification, erasure, and embellishment. In other words, an ideal abode for human beings. (The ineffable bliss we experience is similar to the effect produced by examining the floor plans of real estate sales brochures.) The point of view of maps is always from above, never sideways (except old maps with perspective drawing of scenery) or from below (even when mortals come up with the idea of drawing a map of the underworld, it must still be viewed from above. It is hard to imagine what it would be like to draw a map of the living from below, from the perspective of the underworld). The posture that maps adopt is always one of looking down from on high.

Borges's story speaks the truth: the map that becomes one with the empire is abandoned by later generations in the wilderness and slowly forgotten. Only fragments survive.

1-1

~

SUBTOPIA

Underground is no less mysterious than undersea, and we have had frequent imaginative accounts of this underground. The Italian novelist Italo Calvino has described in *Invisible Cities* the existence of an underground world that corresponds geometrically with the cities aboveground. In fact, however, the underground is not an untrodden realm; for example, the remains of an underground city built more than two thousand years ago by early Christians escaping from persecution can be found in the remarkable stony landscape of Cappadocia in Turkey. Yet to be underground means to be cut off from growth, shut up in murmurs of funereal songs under the heavy soil. It is a city of the banished, an abode for the dead. It can assert its existence only in the form of a grave, like the ancient tomb dating from the Eastern Han dynasty at Lei Cheng Uk Village in Kowloon.

It is not without reason that maps can be regarded as a kind of ancient tomb. The oldest surviving Chinese maps based on actual surveying are those excavated in 1973 at the Han dynasty Tomb No. 3 at Mawangdui in Wulipai in the eastern suburbs of Changsha in Hunan. There are three maps painted on silk in 168 B.C.E.: one topographical map, one showing garrisons, and one showing towns. If ancient tombs are places buried underground, then, as referential objects pointing toward immaterial ideas, maps are places buried under time. The act of reading an ancient map is inevitably a process of unearthing, for every ancient map is bound to be covered by another more recent one. At the moment of completion, or even before that, a map is in reality already in the past, because no map can be synchronous with time. A map is time frozen, but it is not the frozen time of any particular moment, for unlike photography, the making of maps cannot be a matter of an instant but has to pass through a period of time pervaded by external change. Therefore, the time immobilized in maps is fictional time that never existed. It follows then that the places depicted by maps are by necessity subtopias.

Take, for example, the Kowloon Peninsula. It is apparent from an eight inch to one mile planning map of Kowloon from 1863 that apart from the southern tip, where some development had already taken place, the rest of the area was covered with hills and fields. The map is monochromatic with the chief topographical features indicated with simple but clear contour lines, its minimalist style seeming to suggest a kind of rustic simplicity. In an 1887 map of Kowloon, the southern half of the peninsula is already covered in a patchwork of yellow, orange, and purple overlaid with minutely delineated streets, as cultivated and uncultivated land alike was slowly covered under strict orderliness. In addition to the gradual encroachment of urban development in the countryside, maps of Kowloon from 1902 to 1924 show layers of superimposition and accumulation over the city area itself, so that Robinson Road, in 1902 the main thoroughfare, had been replaced by Nathan Road by 1924. In an eight-inch map dating from 1947, the age-old simplicity of the Kowloon Peninsula is completely hidden under densely woven lines. It had become the sediment of time, the subtopia that can only be remembered and imagined, issuing faint, distant whispers from beneath layers of signs similar to geological strata.

12

TRANSTOPIA

The earth gives us a consoling feeling of permanence. Rivers change course or silt up, oceans swallow people up or set them adrift, and islands become detached. Only the earth remains impressively steady, seemingly unchanging throughout the ages. Apart from earthquakes, the earth is almost completely reliable, but it is also stagnating and dull. As scholars of cartography, we cannot cast off the ancient (and even banal) affection that people generally feel toward the earth, yet we are nevertheless intent on finding a way to introduce change to its steadfast immobility.

A map is one way of changing the earth. I suspect that it is also the most effective, thorough, and meaningful way. This change can take at least two different forms: transformation and transference. The former tackles the earth's solidity, the latter its weight. Each involves a different feature of maps. The former is related to the technical aspects of drawing maps, while the latter relates to their material existence: whether a print, an engraving, or a stone rubbing, they are tangible, portable, foldable, and disposable, they can be circulated and they can be damaged.

The unique contribution of mapmaking is its ability to distort the earth's solidity. The scale and degree of this distortion could probably be matched only by another global movement of the earth's crust. Before the development of scientific mapmaking, the work of distorting the earth had been done in an impromptu and imaginative way. (Of course, there had been no lack of boring stuff, like the stereotyped representations of the world with Jerusalem as its center in the medieval *orbis terrae* maps configured under Christian ideology.) Following the advancement of scientific surveying in the seventeenth and eighteenth centuries, distortions entered into the phase of systematization as different methods of projection allowed great flexibility in regard to position, area, and distance. The landform on the map can be elongated, flattened, enlarged, or reduced in size. For example, in a world map drawn with Mercator's right-angled cylindrical projection, the bearings of two points are the same as in the real world, but as areas become larger on the map the farther away from the equator they are, the distance between the points increases with the result that the size and shape of the northern and southern polar regions are highly distorted.

This technical transformation is no doubt only symbolic. After all, nobody can create a global disaster simply by scribbling on maps. But the opposite is also true. Symbols often take the place of reality and become people's only means of perception. When people place their trust in maps without reserve, their cognitive receptivity will also become unconsciously flexible. Therefore, even though Antarctica may appear as small as Australia or bigger than Africa as a result of different methods of projection, people will still be satisfied with its indication as Antarctica and pay no heed to its transformations.

Apart from the question of transforming the earth by means of different techniques, I have also spent some time contemplating the question of its weight. The subject of my research is, how can a place be transferred? Or maybe a more fundamental question is, what does transference mean? The ultimate answer appears disappointingly ordinary, but its truth cannot be overlooked. Transference means to put something from one hand into another hand, that is, to hand over. In fact, it is extremely simple to transfer a place: you need only hand over a map of the place. The earth loses its weight, becoming unbearably light. On maps, places become transferable objects, concrete minimized versions of the vast, incomprehensible earth. When you hold this feather-light map in your hands, you are grasping the earth. In ancient times, Jing Ke made an attempt on the King of Qin's life under the pretext of presenting him with a map: as the map unrolls, the dagger is disclosed. The symbolic meaning here is worth pondering. Yet when for whatever reason you acquire or lose a map through an act of transfer, you may not be sure of what is being handed over, whether it is the place itself or its sovereignty, knowledge, fantasy, or memory.

The history of mapmaking is full of instances where places are constantly shifting. Take, for example, Hong Kong. You can find traces of its transfer in maps of Hong Kong from 1842, 1861, and 1898. Using a linear symbol known as a boundary as indicator, these maps record continual acts of transference. Not only that, they also delineate the orbit of transfer and even calculate the precise route and date of retrocession. Like stargazers seeking a rare glimpse of Halley's Comet, which appears only once every seventy-six years, people will turn their eyes to the sky on July 1, 1997, and the inhabitants of this land will slowly descend, huddled together on a map like travelers on a flying carpet.

The study of transference in Hong Kong maps inspires me to fresh thoughts on the concept of transtopia. I realize that besides meanings of transformation and transference, it also implies the idea of transit. Places that exist in the form of maps are inevitably fated to suffer transformation and transference, and as such they are like comets that travel unceasingly, circling over and over again, forever in the act of transit, never arriving at their destinations.

Transtopia is a place with transit itself as its destination.

13

MULTITOPIA

Theorists still disagree on the usage of the term "multitopia." Some think that it should be used to indicate multiple spaces created in maps. Take, for example, the 1958 "Hong Kong Street Guide" by the publisher Jan Jan. Thirteen frames of different sizes and shapes are juxtaposed on this map, displaying the maze of streets in each district on Hong Kong Island. The peculiar thing about this juxtaposition is that the relative positions, distances, and areas of the districts have been completely rearranged, and in the resulting confusion Shek Tong Tsui and Kennedy Town, originally on the northern coast of the western district of Hong Kong Island, now appear at the foot of the southwestern side of Victoria Peak, while the coastal area from Causeway Bay to Happy Valley moves to the southeast of Central District.

The multitopia as represented on the Jan Jan map has the following features: first, districts appear side by side without any linkage between them. Cases of sudden transgressions of one space into another also occur frequently in multitopias. For example, while you are walking past Murray Barracks along Queen's Road Central, you may inadvertently stumble into the Causeway Bay Typhoon Shelter; or, when you want to walk toward Shau Kei Wan in the northeast, you may accidentally cross into Aberdeen to the south. In short, this is a characteristic of collage. Second, districts overlap. For example, Hong Kong Island and Kowloon appear in

Mid-Levels, while the northern coast of Hong Kong Island and part of Victoria Harbor are overlaid on the waters of Victoria Harbor to the north of Central. Third, the "same" districts appear side by side in different scales. For example, Central appears with the highest frequency, in scales of 1:4,500, 1:6,650, 1:17,500 and in an unspecified smaller scale, separately located in the upper, middle, lower, and bottom left parts of the map. In other words, this is a city that incorporates spatial configurations of different dimensions. You may be a dwarf at one end of the city but a giant at another. If you find the Central of 1:6,650 too crowded, you can choose to have a stroll in the Central of 1:4,500. The multitopia in the Jan Jan map is an open place, welcoming choice and inviting the unexpected.

Some hold a different view, namely that multitopia is the exact opposite of multiplicity and means mass replication. This happens when the scientific production of maps has developed into printing on a large scale. Before then, every map was a unique, handcrafted product. Many ancient maps found by archaeologists have this character: they are original texts of unquestionable status, elevated above mere instrumentality, and are therefore self-referential and self-sufficient works of art. But the ancient worship of original texts is already out of tune with the times, and the mysterious skills of original mapmaking have been lost. Amid the innumerable simulacra in front of our eyes, no map reading can ever take us back to our old hometown. We are lost in an orderly world, for we cannot go anywhere but along designated pathways. The way I take is no different from yours. Unwilling though we may be, deliberately choosing divergent paths, we are bound to end up at the same spot, on a topography that can be envisaged and comprehended in full.

In an age of scientific surveying and mass production of maps, nobody can escape from the hall of endless mirrors that is multitopia. All we can do is to repeat the same gestures as our own reflections.

14

UNITOPIA

Like multitopia, unitopia is a controversial concept. Unitopia can be understood in opposite ways: first, as an independent place, from the word "unique"; second, as a unified place, from the idea of "unity." The former signifies an individual's self-definition, the latter, the whole swallowing up the individual; the former tends toward division and autonomy, the latter toward convergence and control.

Some people understand the dual meanings of unitopia through concepts of scale and borders. First, the existence of a place on a map is entirely reliant on the boundaries created by borders. A border is the cognitive frame for the division between inside and outside. It is said that the ancient Chinese character for the word "map" is composed of a square frame around the figure of a moving man, meaning "someone in the act of observing or surveying a plot of land." Taking away the border and adding the character for "district" to the right of the man transforms this character into its opposite, a compound character with the meaning "rustic" or "outlying district." This demonstrates the decisive realistic function and symbolic meaning of the map border in terms of cultural-geographical perception. The border endows the place it encloses with independence in regard to the outside and unity in regard to the inside. It rejects "whatever is not this place" and embraces "everything that belongs to the place." Therefore, the map border is a manifestation of the dual meaning of unitopia.

The problem is that maps under normal conditions have limited flexibility in terms of size: borders cannot be expanded or contracted indefinitely, so the exclusiveness and inclusiveness of frames have to be regulated by scale. Supposing that the borders and area of a map remain fixed, different scales can enable the frame to perform different defining functions. Since we know that independence and unity, or division and convergence, are for unitopia two sides of the same coin, the rejection or inclusion caused by adjusting the scale can only be a matter of tendency. For example, a 1:10,000 map of Hong Kong demonstrates, on the one hand, the inner unity of the city (including Hong Kong Island, Kowloon, and the New Territories and Outlying Islands), while on the other hand demarcating the independence of Hong Kong as a place that is not "the same as any other place" (for the moment leaving aside in which aspect this is the case). However, when we readjust the scale to 1:15,000,000, Hong Kong becomes a barely discernible dot on a map of the whole of China. Here, the change in scale deprives Hong Kong of its independence and enforces China's unity.

Therefore, all maps are unitopias. Two opposing forces operate within their borders: coming from one direction is an impulse toward small scale, which is also a desire to control the whole world; from the other direction is the ultimate quest for large scale, that is, the impossible task of making a 1:1 map. The latter does not seek comprehensiveness but specificity. Take, for example, a map of Hong Kong and magnify the district called Mong Kok, then the street called Cedar Street, a building on the street, an apartment in the building, a room in the apartment, a desk in the room, the person sitting in front of the desk, the pen in the person's hand and the piece of paper in front of him, and the 1:1 projection of fantasy on this piece of paper.

This is an image of individual autonomy made possible for me by a map on a 1:1 scale with a three feet by three feet square border. It is my personal unitopia on paper.

15

OMNITOPIA

The place that I have never succeeded in finding is omnitopia. In the eleventh century, the monk Heinrich of Mainz (1021–1063), in an essay on religion and geography, quoted the concept of "omnitopia" allegedly taken from the ninth book of *Geographia* by the Greek scholar Ptolemy (90–168).

Ptolemy's monumental work consists of eight books in total. It deals with techniques of mapmaking and theories of projection, lists the longitude and latitude bearings of eight thousand place-names, and includes a world map and twenty-six regional maps. In his map of the world, the longitudes and latitudes are drawn as curved lines in order to rectify the distortion of the earth's curvature when projected on a flat surface. Ptolemy's maps have all been lost; the earliest extant manuscript of his world map is a reconstruction dating from 1561. As for the extra book, that is, the ninth volume, it remains pure hearsay, as Heinrich's essay is the only document we have that quotes directly from it. Europe was then in the dark ages: for having challenged the credibility of the Christian *orbis terrae* map and proposing the concept of omnitopia, Heinrich was accused of heresy and burned at the stake. Along with his life, his essay was also reduced to ashes, its surviving contents scattered among the writings of Renaissance scholars.

Since it is impossible to trace the idea of the omnitopia to its origin, we can only make conjectures based on its literal meanings. The first part, "omni," leads to associations with "omniscient," "omnipotent," and "omnipresent." This allows the bold postulation that omnitopia is a place where nothing is secret, hidden, or overlooked; where nothing is impossible; and where there are no barriers or limitations in time and space. In other words, it is a "total" place, with no leakage, no outside, and no opposite. Since the meaning of "total" must be monistic, its self-contradictions inevitably make it untenable, for it has to include within itself its own boundary, and in this act of inclusion it is bound to create new boundaries. The outside of total is forever an even bigger total, ad infinitum.

There is perhaps another explanation that is more direct (and although it appears superficial, its meaning is in fact profound), that is, to interpret omnitopia as a comprehensive, total map. Imagined in the abstract, an omnitopia is a place that theoretically includes all places. Imagining such a place can be realized only through mapmaking, especially atlases. In other words, it is the ultimate fantasy of a map or atlas encompassing all geographical facts. I thus infer that in the supposedly long-lost ninth book of Ptolemy's *Geographia*, there must be an elucidation of the concept of omnitopia, along with an insanely arrogant and wholly unrealistic practical application: a total map that represents all existing and possible landforms in the entire world.

Cartographic circles, however, must see such a conjecture about Ptolemy's work as a blasphemy against the fine tradition of scientific surveying and mapmaking. To picture the great mapmaker of the Greco-Roman world (who is also a pioneer in the history of world cartography) as a maniac suffering from delusions is the height of impertinence. It also shows ignorance and disrespect toward the cultural heritage of Greek civilization in astronomy, geography, and mathematics. We may wonder if the first to lose his reason was Heinrich, who chanted hymns as the flames consumed him. He was sentenced to death because of his belief that omnitopia was God's vision of the world. The more important background factor, however, was his conviction that man could achieve God's vision through reason and science, and that the communion of vision thus achieved was entry into paradise. Omnitopia, in the end, is a geographic synonym for paradise.

Unconsciously we have always yearned to be one with God. A map is no longer a utilitarian instrument but an epistemological translation of our knowledge of the world. The translated text will ultimately replace the limited vision of our individual selves, becoming a panoramic virtual space in our psyche and spirit, unfolding within our minds a total map that stretches into infinity. In this way we transcend ourselves and lose ourselves, for we are everywhere and nowhere.

It is said that at the moment of death, Heinrich did not falter for an instant in praise of God, the omniscient, omnipotent, and omnipresent.

PART TWO

The City

16

MIRAGE: CITY IN THE SEA

The legendary city of Victoria was, like Venus, born from the waves of the sea. It is not known how it disappeared in the end. The legend thus brings us face-to-face with an archaeological question: by what means can we verify a city's existence?

Suppose we have in hand only fragments of accounts written on this city, which taken together cannot be regarded even as a history; suppose we succeed in collecting items alleged to be its remains from all over the world, including wigs, cheap watches, fake high fashion goods, and retouched landscape postcards; yet so long as we cannot find in the boundless ocean the island on which this city was once built, we cannot rule out the possibility that people systematically wove a web of deceit around it, created counterfeit documents, and forged a nonexistent past.

A map is no different. The remaining maps of Victoria, which vary in quality but abound in quantity, are no guarantee of the city's existence. On the contrary, they throw doubt on its stability and actuality. Reading them is like tracing a lover's inner topography. Under those oscillating, ambiguous, indefinite, and yet suggestive expressions, the map reader's knowledge and imagination are led into a meandering narrative, out of which is woven a novel full of prejudice, jealousy, misunderstanding, perplexity, anxiety, and ecstasy.

It is said that the island on which this city had been situated was barren and uninhabited. It was located off the southern coast of the Chinese mainland, to the east of the former Portuguese colony of Macao. The maps produced by the Qing dynasty court and its local administration from the fifteenth to the end of the nineteenth century testify that the island appeared and disappeared many times for unknown reasons.

The name of what was said to be a neighboring island called Tai Kai Shan (later known as Tai Yue Shan in Cantonese and Lantao Island in English) was recorded on the "Map of Zheng He's Voyages," collected by Mao Kun and reproduced by his grandson, Mao Yuanyi, in 1621. The first time the name Hong Kong appeared was on the "Coastal Map of Guangdong" drawn by Guo Fei in the late sixteenth century. "Hong Kong" never appeared again until the mid-nineteenth century but was replaced by the name Hung Heung Lou Shan (red incense burner mountain) or Hung Heung Lou Shun (red incense burner guard post) in maps drawn by the Chinese. Tradition has it that the British were the first to refer to the whole island as Hong Kong, for in the early days when British sailors fetched water on the south side of the island, the local people told them in their Tanka dialect that the name was Hong Kong (although in fact this name referred only to a nearby village). Another theory maintains that the name came from the production and export of incense in the region, in which, in those days, a tree called *kuan-heung* was extensively cultivated. There are others who believe that the island did not even exist before the arrival of the British, and that the tale of sailors inquiring about the name was pure fiction.

After Guo Fei's "Coastal Map of Guangdong," the island made its appearance in maps attached to documents like *A Record of the Countries of the Sea* (1774), by Chen Lunjiong, *Gazetteer of San-on*

County (1819 edition), and *Guangdong Provincial Gazetteer* (1864 edition), all under the name Hung Heung Lou. That name, however, is completely absent in other contemporaneous maps like the "Area Map of Guangzhou Prefecture" in the imperial encyclopedia *Synthesis of Books and Illustrations Past and Present* (1723), *Atlas of China in the Qianlong Reign* (1769), and Magistrate Chen's "Map of the Waterways of Guangdong," nor was there any mark to indicate the island's existence. In "Map of the Waterways of Guangdong," for instance, one can see the names of places near Hong Kong, such as Kowloon Police Post, Tuen Mun Guard Post, Tai Yue Shan Fort, Cheung Chau, Tseung Kwan O, Tai O, and Kat O, but there is no trace of Hung Heung Lou, and there is only a small island named Chek Chue near its supposed location.

Hung Heung Lou was for several hundred years visible at some times and at other times invisible. Some say that the actual existence of Hung Heung Lou began when Captain Belcher drew his nautical chart of Hong Kong in 1841. From then on, the small island was officially called Hong Kong, and with the exception of the continuous development of the city on its northern coast, the name, shape, and position of the island remained unchanged until recent speculations about its resubmergence. So if map readers today attempt to unearth the remains of the city of Victoria in the vast ocean of maps, what they are after might possibly be to perpetuate a love story born of imagination.

MIRAGE: TOWERS IN THE AIR

A description of Victoria can be found in the book *The Shipwreck of Kino from Bishu*.

In August 1841, a Japanese seaman by the name of Kino set off from Toba for Edo on the ship *Eiju Maru*, a vessel that could carry a load of 1,000 piculs and had sails measuring seventy-four feet. A storm at a far-off sandbank in midjourney broke the mast so that the ship drifted out to sea. After a hundred days adrift on the open sea, the entire crew of thirteen men were rescued by the Spanish ship *Esperanza* and taken to California in the United States. After many twists and turns, Kino was finally able to get passage to Macao on a Portuguese vessel and then left Macao by way of Hong Kong to make his way north along the coast to return to his own country. Kino arrived back in Japan in 1846, but, on suspicion of having violated the policy of national seclusion, he was detained and interrogated. He was finally released and returned to his home district of Bishu. The frontier defense authorities then sent officers to make a second investigation, and they made a record of what he had seen and heard in foreign countries. This became the text that is now included in the *Edo Anthology of Stories of Shipwrecks*.

Here follows an excerpt from *The Shipwreck of Kino from Bishu* concerning Victoria. Implausible passages in the text may be due to Kino's blurred memory or the result of the investigators' fertile imaginations.

To the east of Macao is a barren island occupied by the British, named Hong Kong. Hong Kong is over twenty *ri* square. Bare hilltops rise 6,000 to 6,200 feet. The harbor faces north and is wide with a narrow entrance. It was afternoon when we sailed into the harbor, and a spring mist obscured the surroundings and created an air of loneliness that made us think that it was truly right to call it a barren island. The ship moved slowly and we could catch indistinct glimpses of several hundred large ships moored in the harbor, including Chinese and foreign merchant vessels and British naval vessels. Everything was still, as if it had been there hundreds of years. As we approached the southern shore of the harbor, the mist was torn apart, there was a great sound of steam whistles, the waves surged, and the ships moved back and forward busily, like suddenly awakened sea creatures. In the swirling fog along the shore, buildings thrust upward and several thousand residences lined the harborside, row upon row of houses of all shapes and sizes. Pushing aside the waves, the slowly emerging buildings reached high up on the steep hillsides. As we drew closer, the seawater seemed to recede from the shoreline, so that an orderly arrangement of streets was revealed, with endless streams of hawkers and fishermen. Everywhere hills had been leveled and large-scale construction was taking place with stone masons, bricklayers, plasterers, carpenters, and coolies numbering in their thousands. The work and activity were a confused and noisy turmoil, like ants building an anthill. Berthing and stepping ashore on that land born of the sea made us feel as if we had been set adrift. The vast space before us created a dreamlike scene like someone lost at sea.

The approximate time of Kino's passage by Victoria would have been March 1845.

POTTINGER'S INVERTED VISION

Of the existing maps of Victoria, "Pottinger's Map" should be the
earliest. This map is said to have been drawn up in 1842 by Sir
Henry Pottinger, the first governor in Victoria. The street plan and
land allotment boundaries on the island's northern shore are all
shown. The design is sketchy but somewhat more careful than a
draft, while its dimensions and topography differ in many places
from later maps of the area.

"Pottinger's Map" is arranged with the south at the top and
must be looked at upside down in order to fit in with our custom-
ary way of reading maps. This may be because it is from the early
period of British occupation. Attention had not yet shifted from
water to land, and since they were facing south from the harbor,
this gave rise to a map layout with land above water. It has been
thought that Sir Henry occasionally suffered from inverted vision.

Some have seen the purpose of the map as a record of the first
lots of land that Captain Charles Elliot, the plenipotentiary and
superintendent of trade in China, sold hastily on the occupation
of Hong Kong. That sale was subsequently not approved and for
a time gave rise to disputes between the colonial government and
traders. Only a small proportion of the lots marked on this map
appear on later maps. However, there is no substantial evidence
to support this idea. If the map was really drawn up by Pottinger

in 1842, it could not be a record of Elliot's land sales, because Pottinger arrived in Hong Kong in August 1841 and took over Elliot's posts as well as being appointed the first governor of Hong Kong, and he would definitely not have made a record of Elliot's "illegal" land sales. This argument is based on the hypothesis that the map was drawn up by Pottinger in 1842. If the hypothesis turns out to be false, another explanation will have to be found.

Notes taken by Pottinger's adjutant, William Hahns, give a completely different version. Pottinger first arrived in Hong Kong on August 21, 1842, to inspect the local construction works. At that time there were as yet no buildings on the island and Queen's Road was still being constructed along the northern shore. Hahns saw Pottinger entering the private part of the governor's mat-shed and studying a sketch map supplied by naval personnel. He did not even bother to listen to reports about inspections of departing troops. The following day, the governor sailed north to take part in the campaign against ports on the China coast. Hahns recalled that during the campaign, Pottinger often found time on the warship to work on a map of the north shore of Hong Kong. From time to time he demarcated bigger and smaller leases along the shoreline, here and there filling in the names of big merchants like Matheson, Jardine, and Dent. He envisaged locations for a post office, land office, and marine office, outlined the scale of Government House, and sketched the long winding line of Queen's Road. In Hahns's words, "Sir Henry Pottinger early on envisaged his queen's city on paper."

On his return to Hong Kong in February 1842, Sir Henry Pottinger discovered that the deputy superintendent of trade, A. R. Johnston, had carried out an unauthorized sale of "public land" at low prices to British merchants and officials and that the lots sold were actually identical to the ones that he had marked out on his map during the military campaign. As a result, Pottinger

PART TWO: THE CITY

overturned the land sale and established new procedures for selling land.

Hahns was accidentally killed by a sailor in a drunken brawl in 1843. He was thirty-five and unmarried and his only possessions were his everyday clothes and several books in which he had scribbled fragmentary notes and poems.

Pottinger spent his early years in India in the service of the East India Company. He had a rich experience of work in the colonies and received a knighthood. When he took part in the Afghan War, his inverted vision made him see in his imagination the enemy fighters as reflections in water.

19

GORDON'S JAIL

"Gordon's Map" of 1843 is mentioned in the documentary records of Victoria. The original is impossible to find, but a still-extant map is said to be a copy. This map presents a general picture of Victoria at its birth and shows the orderly arrangement of the buildings lining Queen's Road following the shore. The map's most notable features are the jail and magistracy on what was then still a bare hillside. They encompassed an area equivalent to several dozen of the buildings along the shore and constituted by far the largest compound.

A. T. Gordon was the first head of the Land Office and subsequently became the first surveyor general in 1843. A large number of sketch maps thought to have been drawn by Gordon in Victoria were discovered among the possessions left behind by Gordon's close associate, the merchant Jeremy Thompson. The sketch maps were kept in a mansion in Kent, England, that belonged to Thompson's descendant Anne Thompson, but the originals were destroyed in a fire in 1945. However, the content of this set of maps can by and large be discerned from Anne Thompson's book *Jeremy Thompson: Merchant Pioneer and Humanist*.[1]

---

[1] The first edition of *Jeremy Thompson: Merchant Pioneer and Humanist* was published in 1934 with a print run of one thousand. Distribution records show that seven copies were sold in all and that the author gave away one hundred twenty copies. It is thought that the remaining

Anne Thompson relates how as a child she won permission from her family to leaf through the sketch maps of her great-grand-father's friend. There were altogether forty-five sheets, all of them depicting construction in the coastal areas of colonial Victoria in southern China. The maps, which were drawn up from February to December 1843, exhibited particularly striking changes in the con-figuration of Victoria Gaol to the south of the area known as Central District. In the first completed maps, Victoria Gaol and Magistrate's Court were already the largest and most spacious landmarks in the city. Victoria Gaol, located on the hillside, subsequently changed its appearance on the maps several times. At times it expanded to the south, climbing up toward Mid-Levels, while at other times it extended north toward the harborside, even to the point of cov-ering the entire Central District commercial area. It also radiated a netlike structure with dotted lines connecting it with the main buildings in Central District, Sheung Wan, and Wan Chai. A map from the end of July placed it on the land at the time occupied by Government House. Finally, in the white margin of the last map, from December 1843, Gordon simply wrote GAOL OF VICTORIA in capital letters, replacing the caption CITY OF VICTORIA. The jail and the city were one and the same.

The British occupied Hong Kong in January 1841, and William Caine was appointed chief magistrate and superintendent of the jail in April the same year. The building was completed by October in an exceptionally short time, and it was the first large-scale public facility to come into use.

---

more than eight hundred volumes were destroyed in the big fire at the country house in Kent. Jeremy Thompson (1795–1866) started out as an opium merchant, later turned to trade in medicines, and was quite a well-known philanthropist.

20

"PLAN OF THE CITY OF VICTORIA," 1889

The 1889 "Plan of the City of Victoria" shows that the city was already quite well developed. The street network extended farther outward from Central District, Sheung Wan, and Wan Chai, reaching Kennedy Town in the west and Causeway Bay in the east, and expanding to the higher levels and the Peak in the south. To the north the shoreline was shifted into the harbor. Looked at from a distance, this monochrome street map resembles a yellowing sketch of the habitat of climbing plants.

The most striking and thought-provoking part of the map is an area to the north outlined with a dotted line along the harborside. If we accept Roland Barthes' reading of photographs as put forward in *Camera Lucida*, we should then not exclude it from map reading. Our eyes are thus often struck by some indescribable *punctum*. It seems to me that the dotted line in the water is such a *punctum*. Even people with a limited understanding of maps know that dotted lines represent the extent of projected reclamation work, that is to say, the direction of the city's future development. This was originally the most superficial and unremarkable meaning of the dotted-line symbol. However, it also added a layer of complexity to the grammar of map language: apart from affirming a perpetual present tense (i.e., repeating over and over to the reader: this is Victoria as it is now in 1889), at the same time it also pointed toward a future tense (i.e., the future Victoria is like this). Inevitably these tenses in the end become part of past time, thereby making it impossible for people to neglect the difference between tense and time. In this difference we can glimpse the city's fictionality.

A "plan" is a plane figure but also a design, a present visualization of future form. On the one hand it does not yet exist and is unreal, but on the other hand it is being designed and will be constructed. A plan is thus a kind of fiction, and the meaning of this fiction is inseparable from the design and blueprint. A fiction is not the same as something completely lacking any connection with reality. On the 1889 "Plan," the road along the northern shore of Victoria is the Praya, but the name was changed to Des Voeux Road on the completion of the harbor reclamation project in 1903, while the new waterfront street was named Connaught Road. Des Voeux Road and Connaught Road are in a distinctive sense fictitious, and Victoria can also be said to be a fictitious city that is continually drawn up with dotted lines on maps, a city forever combining the present, future, and past tenses. If you compare a map of Victoria from the 1840s with one from 1996, you will be amazed to see that the city is so fictitious that it easily matches the most unrestrained novel. The dotted lines are still being extended like a never-finished story.

Fiction is the essential character of Victoria and even of all cities, and city maps are by necessity novels expanding, altering, embellishing, and repudiating themselves.

2-1

THE FOUR *WAN* AND NINE *YEUK*

In 1903 the Hong Kong government published the boundaries of the city of Victoria in the government gazette and set up six boundary stones. These stones are said to have been located in the following places: (1) in a waterfront park north of Victoria Road, (2) opposite St Paul's Primary School in Wong Nai Chung Road, (3) in Bowen Road about a third of a mile from its junction with Stubbs Road, (4) where Tregunter Path meets Old Peak Road, (5) in Hatton Road 1,300 feet from Kotewall Road, (6) on the pavement of Pok Fu Lam Road near lamppost 3987.[2]

Chinese residents in the area had different ways of demarcating the boundaries of Victoria, referring to the city as the four *wan* and the nine *yeuk*, literally "the four rings and nine neighborhoods." The four *wan* were Ha Wan, or Lower Ring (i.e., Wan Chai, from Wan Chai Road to Arsenal Street), Chung Wan, or Central Ring (i.e., Central District, from the Murray Barracks Parade Ground to the junction of Wellington Street and Queen's Road Central), Sheung Wan, or Upper Ring (from the junction of Wellington Street and Queen's Road Central to the Government Civil Hospital), and Sai Wan or Western Ring (Connaught Road West to Kennedy Town).

---

[2] *Si huan jiu yue (City of Victoria)* (Hong Kong: Hong Kong Museum, Sep. 1994), 7–8. This source is no longer extant.

There is as yet no accepted explanation of the reason for naming the four districts "rings." Some understand "ring" as meaning "encircling," that is to say an area that is surrounded. To be surrounded can further be understood as either of two opposites: "protected and immune to outside attack" or "beleaguered and with no escape." No matter how it is explained, "ring" in this sense has an inward-looking point of view with focus on its own area. Conversely, some also understand "rings" as links in a chain-shaped relationship, that is to say a chain of interlocked rings. The districts become joined and closely tied together to the point that they are one another's fetters, depending on as well as holding back one another. This is an external means of definition by creating meaning out of the relationships with other districts. Yet a third explanation is that "ring" stands for "cycle" or "period." The "Four Rings" are thus a city that has undergone four cycles of change. So far no one has been able to verify or induce the rules governing its cyclical change, nor has anyone been able to explain the fact that, in addition to the perfect three-phase cycle of "upper," "central," and "lower," there has also emerged the irregular "west" element. The post–New Age cartographic school who lay claim to be heirs to the Chinese tradition of geomancy insist that there is a profound spiritual mystery therein.

The nine *yeuk* are in the main explained by the old assertion that *yeuk* is a territorial division, close in meaning to "district." The word *yeuk* has a specific sense of contract, agreement, or promise, that is to say, a formula for setting boundaries that is recognized by all parties. Some very meticulous textual researchers also feel that we must not neglect the fact that *yeuk* has the additional meaning of "about" or "around." Thus they reach the conclusion that *yeuk* boundaries were approximate, ambiguous, and imprecise, something that has given rise to a debate about Chinese habits and the nature of the Chinese cultural tradition.

In his book *Legends from the Four Wans and Nine Yeuks*, the Englishman Norman Elton quoted what a local fortune-teller and letter writer by the name of Lam Kat had to say about the origin of the name the "nine *yeuk*." A girl from the village of So Kon Po walked every day from east to west through the city to take a lunch basket for her father, who worked in a slaughterhouse in Kennedy Town. On her way through Sheung Wan she would always buy a steaming hot bun from the Tak Hing Tea House in Bonham Strand. A young waiter in the teahouse came to adore this girl and one day made an appointment to meet with her in the afternoon by the harbor in front of the infectious diseases hospital in Kennedy Town. However, something happened that made him fail to keep his appointment, so the next day he came to a new agreement with the girl to meet outside the Kam Ling Restaurant in Shek Tong Tsui. By unhappy coincidence the boy was again unable to make the appointment, and the two of them then changed the place of their rendezvous to the Government Civil Hospital in Sai Ying Poon. The same thing happened again and again as the couple made a series of appointments to meet in several places from east to west: the Tin Tin Hotel in Connaught Road West, Western Market, Central Market, Arsenal Street, and Wan Chai Road. For all sorts of reasons the boy always failed to meet the girl. On the ninth day, finally, the girl agreed to meet the boy at Goose Neck Bridge in Ha Wan but warned him that he must on no account break his promise again. The boy swore by high heaven that he would not do so, but afterward he bumped into a British sailor on the street and was beaten, and by the time he reached Goose Neck Bridge, the girl had thrown herself into the water and drowned.

The "Nine Yeuk" thus means the "Nine Agreements," that is, nine failed appointments in nine different neighborhoods.

22

∽

THE CENTAUR OF THE EAST

In his *El libro de los seres imaginarios* (*The Book of Imaginary Beings*) Borges made an acute observation: the centaur of Western mythical zoology is the most harmonious of all creatures, but its heterogeneous character is often overlooked. Its heterogeneity lies in the fact that it consists of two separate and distinct halves joined (or juxtaposed) together to form a seamless perfection: its human part possesses purely human characteristics, and its animal part is a perfect configuration of a horse. Chinese mythology has no analogous example of a fantastic creature composed of two different parts. Although Chinese imaginary creatures are often made up of parts of different animals, these are amalgamations of many individual features rather than simple combinations of two parts. For instance, the Queen Mother of the West is described in "The Classic of the Western Mountains" (a chapter in *The Classic of Mountains and Seas*) as having a human shape, a leopard's tail, tiger's teeth, and the ability to roar.

There has long been a debate about the proper way to decipher maps of Victoria: is it a case of joining or mixing together? The former seems particularly suited to reading early maps of Victoria, such as the street map of 1889, where it is already possible to discern an obvious dividing line between Central District and Sheung Wan. With the exception of a few streets that run east to west (Bonham

Strand, Queen's Road, Hollywood Road, and Wellington Street) and connect these districts, Central and Sheung Wan present entirely different aspects. The Central District streets almost invariably have English names after people involved in the early development of Victoria (for example, Pottinger Street, named after the first governor, Sir Henry Pottinger; D'Aguilar Street, named after the general officer commanding of the early years, Major-General D'Aguilar; Aberdeen Street, named after the British foreign secretary of the 1840s, Lord Aberdeen, and so on). However, most streets to the west of Tai Ping Shan in Sheung Wan have Chinese names (Po Hing Fong, Po Yan Street, Wing Lok Street, and so forth). Documentary evidence indicates that Pottinger Street also marked a boundary in architectural style, with Central District having British-type buildings and Sheung Wan Chinese-type housing. Seen from the harbor, it must have appeared as a juxtaposition of heterogeneity.

This view has been rejected as a simplification not in keeping with the facts. Cartographers have put forward all sorts of quantitative analysis and location and density data to explain that there was by no means a sharp line dividing eastern and western halves in Victoria. They have attempted to portray the city as a product of mixed blood ties, tangled up and impossible to dissolve—a hybrid. This traditional Queen Mother of the West paradigm held sway for a time, but the view of juxtaposed and coexisting halves still held a certain attraction among scholars. That is why some people still insist that Victoria is the "Centaur of the East."

Borges also summarizes the fifth book of Lucretius's *De rerum natura* (*On the Nature of Things*): The centaur is an impossible creature, for the horse reaches maturity before the human. By the age of three a horse is already full-grown, while a human is a child barely weaned. A horse's life span is also fifty years shorter than a human being's.

23

SCANDAL POINT AND THE MILITARY CANTONMENT

The intentions of the military authorities become quite clear in an 1880 map showing Victoria's military installations. The map represents the district later called Admiralty. Murray Battery is to the left, on a hillside below Government House, and Murray Parade Ground is on a low slope northeast of the battery. Murray Barracks is to the east of the parade ground, on the other side of a road. On a knoll farther east from Murray Barracks stands the building known as Flagstaff House, which was the residence of the general officer commanding. The Naval Yard occupies the central portion of the waterfront and farther east are the Military Hospital and Wellington Battery. Victoria Barracks and the Arsenal are on the hillside south of the hospital, to the right on the map.

We can see that the garrison in Victoria was of a respectable size just from the overall positioning of the military installations. Historical records show that there was a dispute between Pottinger, the first governor, and the military in the early days of the city's construction. Pottinger had originally intended to set aside Western District for military use (i.e., the area to the west of what was later named Possession Point, where British forces first landed on Hong Kong Island), but the military insisted on being stationed in the heart of the city and demanded the use of the hillside in the center (i.e., the area afterward used for the Botanic Gardens and Government House). The dispute eventually had to be taken to

London. The result was that the military cantonment was established to the east of the central area, on a portion of land commanding strategic control over the key east-west main thoroughfare along the northern shore.

These are the facts that we learn from historical and anecdotal sources. Later map researchers arrived at an entirely different conclusion by studying this map. They argued that the layout of military installations in early Victoria had come about as an encirclement of Scandal Point. This map has the place known as Scandal Point right in the middle, south of the naval dockyard, on the low hill between the residence of the general officer commanding and Victoria Barracks. The military installations in this area surrounded Scandal Point to the east, west, and north, as if Scandal Point was the center that the cantonment was designed to protect.

The name Scandal Point was given to the place by the British, although, strictly speaking, "scandal" here should be understood as referring only to malicious gossip. While it is impossible to trace the actual origin of this name, Ye Lingfeng points out in his book *Momentous Changes in Hong Kong History* that Scandal Point was adjacent to St John's Cathedral in Garden Road and the foreign believers who worshipped there on Sundays walked along the short road at Scandal Point on their way back to their Mid-Levels homes. While walking it was natural for them to exchange news and gossip, spreading stories of adultery and scandalous behavior or telling jokes about social events. Although this interpretation of the name seems reasonable, it lacks a substantial foundation.

Some teleological map readers maintain that the relationship between Scandal Point and the surrounding military cantonment was not fortuitous. The function of the cantonment was clearly protecting the scandals while at the same time containing them. By concealing them behind armed fortifications, wider dissemination was prevented, but their continued multiplication was ensured.

24

MR. SMITH'S ONE-DAY TRIP

The central area of Victoria in the early twentieth century is described by the Englishman John Smith (1850–1914) in his book *Round the World on the Sunrise*. His account is useful for our understanding of a map from 1905, which is called "Massey's Directory" and was printed privately by W. S. Bailey & Co. The area covered stretches from the junction of D'Aguilar Street and Queen's Road in the west to the cricket club between Queen's Road and Chater Road in the east and from Ice House Street and Battery Path in the south to Connaught Road and the newly reclaimed waterfront in the north.

The ocean liner SS *Sunrise* sailed from England by way of the Mediterranean to the British colonies of India and Singapore, finally arriving in the city of Victoria on August 9, 1907. The *Sunrise* arrived late and stayed for only one day because of a previous delay caused by a typhoon in the Strait of Malacca. It then continued its journey to northern China and Japan. Smith's account describes how a sampan, "bizarre, filthy and with the flavour of the Orient," took him ashore at Blake Pier. Upon disembarking, he and his party moved on to Pedder Street opposite the pier. At the corner of Des Voeux Road they found a Chinese man, "gaunt, shifty-eyed, speaking English like a pelican singing," who served as their guide. After being shown the building of Jardine, Matheson & Co., they went to have lunch at the Hong Kong Hotel near the junction of Pedder

Street and Queen's Road. The people in Mr. Smith's party found the hotel, which was so famous in the city, to be too old-fashioned, and it had also lost its former view of the harbor after the latest land reclamation. Moreover, "the Chinese hotel waiters appeared so tense all the time that nobody felt very relaxed." Only the hydraulic lift in the lobby was impressive.

After lunch Mrs. Smith and some of the other ladies decided that a visit to a hairdresser was needed after several days of stormy weather at sea and chose to go to Campbell, Moore & Co. on the ground floor of the hotel. Being thoroughly fed up with the Chinese guide's poor English, Mr. Smith also decided to leave the party "in a reckless spirit of exploration." He described himself as "just like an explorer entering a tropical rain forest, a hunting rifle in hand and with dangers on all sides." His sharp eyes swept across the extraordinary creatures in the street, such as "Chinese coolies and chair bearers, all looking the same to me," and some "natives in European attire looking like dressed-up monkeys." Mr. Smith ventured across the busy street with caution and escaped into the post office on the opposite side, where he mailed a letter for his children at home. In lopsided handwriting, this letter, composed on board, recounted his observations on the journey in a style replete with British wit. Turning next into a street named Queen's Road, he soon arrived at Kelly & Walsh, where he shopped for Capstan Navy Cut tobacco, a local map, and books to relieve the tedium on the remainder of the journey. He spent quite some time in the shop reading with great interest such books as *Cantonese Made Easy*, *Gems of Chinese Literature*, and *The Dragon: Image and Demon*. In the end he purchased Herbert A. Giles's *Strange Stories from a Chinese Studio* in two volumes at a price of $6.50. A short distance farther on, Mr. Smith bought seasickness medicine and a bottle of Scotch whisky from A. S. Watson & Co. At the Afong Studio in Ice

House Street he selected a few pictures of local people and scenery that his wife would be bound to treasure, among them a color photograph of a small boy from a poor family carrying a baby on his back. It stirred in him a feeling of being "deeply touched by human sincerity."

After admiring the City Hall and Hongkong and Shanghai Banking Corporation buildings with their elegant colonnades and portals in traditional European style, Mr. Smith felt that he had had a rewarding excursion and rejoined his wife and the other members of their party at the Hong Kong Hotel. They dined at the hotel and then returned to the *Sunrise* by sampan. Mrs. Smith had gained a favorable impression of Victoria, her only disappointment being that she had failed to see the slanting eyes that so many pictures of Chinese people had led her to expect.

Mr. Smith's book includes a sketch map of the central area of Victoria drawn by his wife, Emily. It would seem to be copied from "Massey's Directory," and on it is traced Mr. Smith's circuitous route on the day of his visit to Victoria.

25

THE VIEW FROM GOVERNMENT HOUSE

The governors of Victoria did not have a permanent office or residence in the early years before Government House was built on Government Hill in 1855. However, an examination of cartographic materials reveals that Government House was still only delineated with dotted lines on a map of the central area dating from 1856, thus raising doubts concerning the exact date of its construction. As regards its location, there is no doubt that it had a commanding position overlooking the entire city. The 1889 "Plan of the City of Victoria" shows the Botanic Gardens on the slope behind Government House. It was popularly known as Ping-tau Fa-yuen, the Commander's Garden. On the lower ground in front of Government House were government offices and the Murray Battery, while the commercial area of Central District with its harbor frontage was slightly farther west. A descent from the northeast would pass St John's Cathedral, the Murray Parade Ground, and the City Hall. We can already see on Lieutenant Collinson's survey map of Hong Kong from 1845 how the planned governor's residence on Government Hill would tower over the city.

The tenth governor (1887–1891), Sir William Des Voeux, described the view from Government House as follows in his memoirs:

Looking out at night from the front gallery of Government House, before the moon had risen, I witnessed an effect which was quite new to me. The sky, though clear of clouds, was somewhat hazy, so that the small-magnitude stars were not visible, though some of the larger ones were plain enough. Beneath, however, the air was quite clear, and consequently, though the vessels in the harbour were invisible in the darkness, their innumerable lights seemed like another hemisphere of stars even more numerous than the others, and differing only as being redder.

For over fifty years, the view from Government House probably remained much the same as described by Des Voeux. Even on maps from the 1940s and 1950s the shoreline right in front of Government House is only slightly extended outward. However, a careful study of a 1990 street map of Central, on a scale of 1:5,000, supplemented by other material, reveals Government House blocked in front by the monstrous, postmodern HSBC headquarters, and, to the right, by the Bank of China Tower, the tallest building in the city. The shoreline has also moved northward a considerable distance, making Government House located inland on this map.

There is no reliable documentation of the view from Government House in later periods. It is alleged that Chris Patten, the last governor (1992–1997), remarked to the gardener at Government House one evening shortly before his departure:

Looking out at night from the front gallery of Government House, before the moon had risen, I witnessed an effect which was quite strange to me. The sky, though clear of clouds, was somewhat hazy, so that the small-magnitude stars were not visible, though some of the larger ones were plain enough. Beneath, however, the air was quite clear, and consequently, though the buildings in the city were invisible in the darkness, their innumerable lights seemed like another hemisphere of stars even more numerous than the others, and differing only as being more dizzying.

26

THE TOAD OF BELCHER'S DREAM

Every city has its creation myth. In January 1841 the HMS *Sulphur* investigated the waters around Hong Kong Island under the command of Captain Edward Belcher. That project represented the last stage of a survey journey around the world undertaken by the *Sulphur* from 1836 to 1842. The resulting "Hong Kong Nautical Chart" was the first scientific survey map with Hong Kong Island as its object and also the first map of Hong Kong under British rule. Later historians of cartography evaluated this chart highly, seeing it as an example of the consistently rigorous approach and precise technique of the British Royal Navy surveyors. Annotations indicate that the surveying work was accomplished on the deck of a wooden sailing vessel with the help of sextant, compass, and lead lines. The drafts were then sent to London for copperplate engraving. The chart shows the coastline of Hong Kong Island and carefully records depths in the surrounding waters, while giving only sketchy information on the land area. In this way "Hong Kong" was born on Belcher's *Sulphur*.

To commemorate this pioneering work of local mapmaking, the government of the newborn city of Victoria named the waters off the island's northwestern part, where the *Sulphur* had been at anchor, Belcher Bay. The strait at the northwestern end of the island was named the Sulphur Channel.

We can still read Belcher's own account in his *Narrative of a Voyage round the World Performed in HMS Sulphur during the Years 1836–1842*. However, Stanley Wells, a student of Hong Kong cartography, has written an article entitled "A Cartographer's Nightmare" in which he quotes a manuscript said to be from Belcher's hand and revealing another side to "the first Hong Kong map."

Wells quotes Belcher:

In the evening after our first landing, we returned to the *Sulphur*, since there was simply no place to stay on the barren island. I was unable to sleep for almost the entire night, just sitting by the porthole looking toward the nearby gunboat *Nemesis*, while invisible in the pitch-black darkness behind me was that land that was to be presented to Her Majesty the Queen. At the approach of dawn I witnessed a strange scene. The darkness gradually gave way, and as the sea reflected a cold, blue light, a gigantic monster emerged from the water. I quickly took up my pen to put down the appearance of that creature on paper, but everything before my eyes was engulfed in its growing shadow. I do not know how much time passed, but as I opened my eyes I found myself lying head down on the table with the early-morning sunrays shining obliquely into my eyes. On the drawing paper unfolded in front of me was a sketch of a jumping toad, its body all covered with warts.

It is said that the above passage was later excised, and it does not appear in the *Narrative of a Voyage round the World*. Belcher subsequently drew his image of Hong Kong Island for "The Hong Kong Nautical Chart" with hachure representation of relief, and Wells describes how that image happens to have an uncanny resemblance to the drawing left on the paper that early morning.

On January 24, 1841, when the negotiations between China and Britain to end the Opium War had not yet reached agreement, the commander of the British expeditionary force, Sir J. G. Bremer, ordered the immediate occupation of Hong Kong Island. Captain Belcher proceeded on the *Sulphur* to the northwestern part of the small island and landed at Possession Point on January 25.

27

THE RETURN OF KWAN TAI LOO

The inhabitants of Victoria could not have foreseen that they would be following the twists and turns of "Kwan Tai Loo." This phrase can be interpreted as "Ah Kwan leading the way" but also as "girdle road." However, what was subsequently renamed Kwan Tai Loo is completely unrelated to the Kwan Tai Loo of old.

Ye Lingfeng has presented a careful study of the origin of the name Kwan Tai Loo in his *Momentous Changes in Hong Kong History*. First of all he has shown that the legend of "Ah Kwan showing the way" is a fantasy concocted by early British colonialists. The story is that a Chinese man by the name of Ah Kwan acted as a guide for the British when they landed and that the route along which he took them came to be known as Kwan Tai Loo. The scene of Ah Kwan guiding the British was subsequently painted and incorporated into the official seal of the city of Victoria as used until 1962.

Ye Lingfeng believes that the Cantonese expression *kwan tai* should instead be understood as the girdle (*tai*) of female attire (*kwan*). In the early days of Hong Kong, a mountain road zigzagged across the center of the island from south to north. As seen from Kowloon across the harbor, it resembled a girdle around the island, and so the villages along a section of the road became known as Kwan Tai Loo (*loo* meaning "road"). This name occurs as early as in the late Ming dynasty edition of the *Dongguan County Gazetteer*, in the taxation section giving the annual levies at different places. In a memorial to the Daoguang emperor during the Opium War, the high imperial official Qishan mentioned "the place locally known as Kwan Tai Loo" when referring to the site of Victoria soon after the British had occupied Hong Kong. The first issue of the government gazette after the founding of the city mentions a village with fifty inhabitants named Kwan Tai Loo. The Chinese characters used for the name in this document mean something like "public highway" and are not the same as those meaning "girdle road" or "Ah Kwan leading the way." However, it must be a case of erroneous transcription of the local name using other characters with the same pronunciation. A search through nineteenth-century maps reveals that maps produced by the Chinese authorities still used the name Kwan Tai Loo for quite some time after the founding of Victoria. Examples of this are the "Map of the Sun-on-district," drawn in 1868 by Simeone Volonteri, and the map included in the *Guangdong Provincial Gazetteer* from as late as 1897, where the simple yet elegant Kwan Tai Loo has survived.

All trace of the name Kwan Tai Loo was erased from twentieth-century maps as Victoria expanded, devouring everything in its path. The modern inhabitants of Victoria had no idea what the name referred to. Some rash and sloppy collectors of old stories made far-fetched or excessively literal interpretations, arguing that the notion of a woman's girdle must have something to do with "petticoat influence" and nepotism, also known as *kwan tai* in Chinese history. In their judgment the term *kwan tai loo* casts aspersions on Chinese social groups as prone to underhand dealings, excluding outsiders, basing influence on kinship ties, and emphasizing personal relations while neglecting legality. It is hard to understand how such baseless lies had come to be accepted as incontrovertible truth toward the end the century and even made some cynics call for the restoration of the name Kwan Tai Loo. Some cartographers predicted that the city would enter a new "Kwan Tai Loo age," and the scholarly journal *Studia Cartographica* published a fashionable computer-generated "déjà-vu topographical chart." The city of Victoria has been renamed Kwan Tai Loo on this chart.

28

THE CURSE OF TAI PING SHAN

Tai Ping Shan (peace mountain) is, strictly speaking, not a mountain but a hillside district in Victoria situated to the south of Sheung Wan between Queen's Road and Caine Road. It was a Chinese residential quarter in the early history of Victoria.

As an age of peace and prosperity began, however, Tai Ping Shan was slowly forgotten, and the name also vanished from maps. The 1889 "Plan of the City of Victoria" shows Tai Ping Shan as a densely built-up area crisscrossed by alleys, but on twentieth-century maps the only signpost that remains to connect people's minds to the past is Tai Ping Shan Street. The most conspicuous landmarks in the vicinity of Tai Ping Shan Street are Blake Garden and the Tung Wah Hospital.

There are somewhat unpleasant stories about Blake Garden's past. It is said that the Chinese neighborhood of Tai Ping Shan lacked proper planning and supervision for several decades after the founding of Victoria, and its inadequate sanitary conditions resulted in an outbreak of plague in 1894. In just a few months, from May to September, there were over twenty-five hundred plague deaths. Since Tai Ping Shan had been the center of the epidemic, the government expropriated the area in 1895, pulled down all the buildings, and rebuilt the district with better sanitary facilities. Blake Garden was subsequently laid out on land between Tai Ping

Shan Street and Po Hing Fong and was named after the governor in whose term of office it was completed. In order to prevent an epidemic from attacking European residential areas, the authorities passed the Peak Reservation Ordinance in 1904 prohibiting Chinese people from settling in the Peak district above 788 feet above sea level.

The sad history of Tai Ping Shan was then buried under the flowers and birdsong of Blake Garden. Giant banyan trees locked in the souls of the dead, their benign roots driving out putrid vapors so that everything implied by the name "Peace Mountain" came true. From then on peace spread as widely as once the plague had done. It eroded the memories of Victoria's inhabitants, while also bequeathing the symptoms of forgetfulness to later generations, so that people eventually began to doubt that Tai Ping Shan had been the home of their forefathers, just as they also failed to realize that many directors of the earliest charitable institution in the entire city, Tung Wah Hospital, had been opium merchants. A small number still obstinately believed in the story of Tai Ping Shan but were no longer able to find any clues to its existence on maps.

An English couple who were fond of keeping parrots are said to have lived in the Mid-Levels district next to Tai Ping Shan when the area was ravaged by the plague. As they had the misfortune to die from infectious disease, their house was seen as unlucky and pulled down, and about a dozen parrots were made homeless. They took shelter in the banyan trees that had been transplanted from elsewhere into the new Blake Garden, where they thrived and multiplied. More than a century later, scholars researching the history of Tai Ping Shan suddenly hit upon the bright idea that generations of Blake Garden parrots might have passed down authentic vocalizations from the past. They went to Blake Garden with audio equipment to interview the birds' descendants, as if recording oral history. It seems that they could just discern monotonously repeated shrieks in the parrots' clamor but were unable to tell whether they were curses or blessings: "Tai Ping! Tai Ping!"

29

WAR GAME

A still-extant map of Victoria designed by the British but printed in color with a Japanese text has frequently been cited as evidence of Japan's unbridled ambitions in East Asia during World War II. The title of the map is "An Outline Map of the Military Installations of Hong Kong," and it was drawn around 1939 or 1940. The map carefully sets out how the garrison was deployed in Victoria and its surrounding area, precisely indicating the locations of army camps, batteries, naval bases, ammunition depots, power plants, oil-storage tanks, and other installations of strategic importance, and also providing an analysis of the effect of the topography and the harbor on military movements.

By the twenty-first century, British scholars referred to this map at international conferences on East Asian history to show that the Japanese army had incontrovertibly attacked Hong Kong in the past. They also supported their arguments by quoting the memoirs of the chief of staff of the 38th Division of the Japanese 23rd Army, which had been given the task of occupying Hong Kong. This officer valued the map highly for its extreme accuracy and "expressed his deep respect" for "the general staff's always thorough reconnaissance." However, another conference participant, the Japanese historian Fujimoto Hiroo, presented counterevidence asserting that the map actually belonged to a

Japanese war game called Attack that was popular in the middle of the twentieth century. The game required a minimum of two players: one designed a strategy for garrisoning and defending a place (usually a city) on the map, while another had to work out the best strategy of attack. The game ended with a judgment by an experienced and strategically knowledgeable third party who determined which scheme was the superior and who was the winner. The game was said to have been tremendously popular among young people and had been strongly promoted by the Ministry of Education as beneficial to intellectual growth and skills among students. Fujimoto traced the origin of this game to the old Chinese expression "paper strategist" and also saw a connection with the computer games that emerged toward the end of the twentieth century, thus verifying that humans have a common and natural psychological desire for imaginary warfare in virtual space. His conclusion was that the occupation of Hong Kong was a reality only in the two-dimensional space of "An Outline Map of the Military Installations of Hong Kong." Fujimoto's arguments met some support among Chinese scholars or else deliberate disregard.

The modern Japanese fiction writer Hiroshi Inoue reminisced about his childhood experiences in an interview:

My seemingly never-ending early childhood was in the late 1930s and early 1940s. Life in our country was extremely difficult at that time, with everything in short supply, but being free from restrictions imposed by older males, I had carefree days and was even bored to the point of feeling gloomy. The quiet lanes often echoed with the hollow broadcast sound of victory bulletins, but my only pastime was drawing maps of nonexisting places on the blank sides of scrap paper. I do not actually understand why maps of all things made such a deep impression on my immature and ignorant mind; in any case, what I first thought of when taking up a pen was not writing words or making pictures but to draw a map. The places I made up may have been carelessly scrawled on paper, but to me they were real and I could see a pattern gradually emerging. In my imagination an island would always appear first, then a peninsula to the north, with a harbor in between. With its eastern and western approaches rather narrow, the harbor was an excellent and well-sheltered anchorage. To the north of the peninsula I placed a range of tall hills that formed a natural barrier and separated the port city on the southern tip of the peninsula and the northern shore of the island from the mainland to the north. I imagined the city to have strong defenses and set up fortifications at every strategic point to guard the entrances to the harbor. I also constructed a defensive line that stretched through the high ground to resist an enemy attack from the north. At every stronghold on my maps I made detailed notations suggesting all kinds of plans for occupying the city. I could often spend the better part of a day amusing myself in this fashion, and it was probably at that time that I first began to develop my creative powers. It was only in the 1960s that I learned that there was such a place as Victoria, and to my surprise the map of that city happened to coincide with the one that the lonely and introspective child had inadvertently made up in his utter boredom. From then on I knew that a fiction writer's greatest nightmare is to discover that nonsense from his own imagination is actually true reality.

PART THREE

Streets

∽

SPRING GARDEN LANE

Spring Garden Lane was one of the oldest streets in Hong Kong. It had already become a settlement for British people on the island when Hong Kong was first opened as a treaty port, and it is said that the first governor's official residence was located on this site. According to research by Ye Lingfeng, the word "spring" in Spring Garden does not refer to the season (as in the Chinese version of the name) but to a water source. Ye quotes a passage in John Luff's *The Hong Kong Story* describing the scene as it looked in the summer of 1841, on the stretch of road going west from Wong Nai Chung on Hong Kong Island:

> On the way, where they are marking out the road, you pass through a most pleasant spot, where a cool spring gushes from the ground. This pleasant spot is quite a contrast with the rest of the waterfront, its richer foliage giving it an almost English appearance. One or two people have it in mind, for the shady trees will form a most welcome garden spot. The spring, gushing cool and sweet from the ground suggests the name its first occupants will bestow upon it: Spring Gardens.

Ye Lingfeng also describes a lithograph by Murdoch Bruce from 1846 called *Spring Gardens*:

The houses are two-story buildings in the tropical colonial style with spacious arcades. A European woman holding a parasol is walking her pet Pekinese down the street. A broad path down the middle has been made for horse riding or light carriages. It shows how prosperous the street was at this time.

This ideal residential environment was originally located at the Praya at the starting point of Queen's Road East, which later became Wan Chai. After more than a century of land reclamation, the later Spring Garden Lane became quite far from the waterfront. There are at least two different versions chronicling the rise and decline of Spring Garden.

Norman Elton's *Legends from the Four Wans and Nine Yeuks* relates the life story of a British merchant, Jonathon Parker. Parker was one of the first to move into Spring Garden in the early years, and it has been said that he gave the place its name. He and his wife, Camille, enjoyed an idyllic existence in Spring Garden, where they gave birth to a son. Parker and his wife lost their lives when they were attacked by local bandits while on a walking trip in the hills near Wong Nai Chung in the summer of 1848. Their relatives took their son back to Britain, and Parker's property in Spring Garden gradually fell into disrepair. Fifty years later, their son, Charles, who had become a successful businessman, returned to Spring Garden, where he put considerable effort into rebuilding the property, restoring Spring Garden to its former glory. Charles married the daughter of a wealthy Chinese merchant, and they resided in Spring Garden for the rest of their lives. Thereafter Spring Garden once again passed from prosperity to decay, and this time its decline was not reversed.

The local historian Lau Tou, however, gave an entirely different account in his *Stories of Hong Kong Streets*:

As the British residents in Hong Kong moved into the cooler areas on the Peak, the area around Spring Garden lost its former gentility. It eventually degenerated into a quarter for low-class prostitutes, known locally as *dai lum-ba* (literally, "big numbers"). These prostitutes, whose clientele was exclusively foreign sailors and seamen, were frequently treated with brutality. A British sailor named Charles, whose nickname was the Avenger, raped and then strangled a Chinese prostitute. After the Hong Kong police authorities issued a warrant for his arrest, his drowned corpse was eventually discovered in the harbor.

In the 1996 street map, Spring Garden Lane is only one of many narrow lanes in the old part of Wan Chai, indistinguishable from nearby Stone Nullah Lane. Spring Garden withered and dried up between these tales of restoration and revenge.

ICE HOUSE STREET

Ice House Street was a hillside road located in Central. Its upper end was connected to Lower Albert Road, and it intersected with Queen's Road at the bottom. Originally there had been an ice warehouse on this street, established in 1845, which imported natural ice blocks from America for consumption by foreigners living in Hong Kong during the summer and to provide cold storage for foodstuffs. It also supplied ice free of charge to local hospitals. Since Queen's Road ran alongside the harbor in those days, it was convenient for ships transporting the ice to unload their cargo for storage at the harborside. The Ice House's business was threatened when a merchant set up a factory for manufacturing ice in Spring Garden in Wan Chai in 1866, and it eventually stopped importing natural ice from overseas in 1880. The Ice House and its competitor, the Hong Kong Ice Company, were both taken over by Dairy Farm in 1918.

As it happens, the Chinese name of the street does not correspond exactly with its English name: pronounced *suet-chong* in Cantonese, it literally means "snow factory." The Chinese word for "ice" is *bing*, but Hong Kong people were in the habit of referring to "ice" as "snow" (*suet*). Another thing is that the "snow factory" was not actually a factory (*chong*) but a godown (*fu*). In short, the correct translation for the English name would have been *bing-fu*.

There is an argument to the contrary, however, according to which the term "snow factory" is an accurate description of the company, or, at least, that manufacturing snow was one of the Ice House's sidelines. According to this claim, the "snow factory" in its early days was investigating how to manufacture snow as well as supplying ice to local residents. This suggests that snow might actually have been manufactured, that is, creating the effect of a mock snowstorm in imitation of the weather conditions in the expatriates' home country. The idea was both to ease the discomfort caused by the summer heat (to which the foreigners found it hard to adjust) and to dispel their homesickness at the lack of a true winter. In this sense, "snow factory" is not a mistranslation but a wholly appropriate term for the enterprise's other function and purpose.

The advantage of "snow factory" as a term, compared with "ice house," is that it actually comes closer to revealing the true nature of colonial society. We have no way of knowing now whether the plan to manufacture snow eventually succeeded, but it was at one time a very agreeable (although secret) custom to go to the Ice House to experience the joys of a chilly European winter. There was supposed to have been a fully furnished Victorian-style living room in the cellar where ladies and gentlemen could sit at their leisure and enjoy the warmth and comfort of afternoon tea around an open fireplace.

In the colony's early days there was a story that circulated widely among the local Chinese that the first act of each new arrival from Britain was to head straight for the Ice House in Central to put their memories and dreams into cold storage in the cellar, lest they rot in the cruel subtropical climate.

Hong Kong people called ice cream snow cake (*suet-gou*). Dairy Farm, the company that took over the Ice House, afterward became a major manufacturer of ice cream. Its depot used to be in Ice House Street, next to the Ice House, and the building afterward became the premises of the Fringe Club, a place where artists could perform their dreams whether sweet and creamy or icy cold.

32

SUGAR STREET

Sugar Street was a short street located between Yee Wo Street (named after Jardine, Matheson & Co., known in Cantonese as the Yee Wo Company) and Gloucester Road in Causeway Bay (although it is so short it seems hardly worth mentioning on a map). There used to be a sugar refinery in the street, hence the name. However, the street also had an unofficial name, Silver Dollar Street, because the refinery's forerunner on the site was a mint. In fact, the interchangeability of coinage and sugar casts an intriguing light on local historical developments.

In 1866, the government invested $400,000 in the construction of the Hong Kong Mint in Causeway Bay to mint its own silver coinage (of the kind in common use in Britain), also reminting on commission new silver dollars in place of the clients' old coins. But the mint did poor business, failing to make a profit, and financial difficulties brought operations to an end in 1868. The plant was sold to Japan for $60,000, and the site was bought by Jardine, Matheson for $60,000 for development as a sugar refinery.

However, there is another version of the mint's closure. According to rumor, a strange event took place when the mint first went into operation. After the workers had poured the molten silver into the casting molds, what emerged at the other end was heaps of sparkling white sugar. The same thing happened continually over the next two years. Reluctant to let it be known and obliged to compensate its clients from its own silver reserves, the government suffered severe financial losses.

This massively extravagant by-product of the mint was initially allocated for internal consumption only, supplied to high officials and departments for use in sweetening their afternoon tea. Later, some of it was also secretly sold on the market or shipped to other British colonies in Southeast Asia, even to Britain itself. There was a somewhat exaggerated claim that Queen Victoria and members of the royal family were particularly fond of sugar produced by the Hong Kong Mint because it represented such high value. Although the side effects of the mint's malfunction were within acceptable boundaries, nevertheless the Hong Kong government in the end closed the mint down, partly because the costs were far too high and also for fear that the truth would leak out.

Commentators believed that selling the mint to Jardine, Matheson was a government cover-up to conceal the scandal; some even believed that Jardine, Matheson had been a partner in constructing the mint in the first place. Once it had bought the mint and ordered the purchase of new machinery, the sugar produced by Jardine, Matheson was sold locally and in China. People have speculated that its sugar trade was enormously prosperous, becoming perhaps its most important source of profits apart from opium. Lo Tung, in his *Record of Strange Happenings in Hong Kong*, quotes a worker at the refinery as saying that every day they would pour the raw materials for refining white sugar into the machines, while what emerged at the other end was a steady stream of sparkling, sweet silver coins.

The refinery was subsequently destroyed in the typhoon of 1874, when the whole plant and warehouse stock were swept out to sea by huge waves. Seamen and fishermen have testified that following the disaster the brackish waters of Victoria Harbor began to taste sweet, and there was also a tendency for fish caught in the harbor to be oversweet and fatty. The refinery was not rebuilt, for reasons that are not clear, and only the name lingered on as witness to its former existence. Lo Tung summed up his narrative with the following enigmatic line in colloquial Cantonese: "That's how it goes: feed them sugar and you feed them shit." It remains unclear whether this is a comment on the ruling strategy of the colonial government in exercising its political and economic powers or on the operation of divine justice.

33

TSAT TSZ MUI ROAD

The story goes that Tsat Tsz Mui Road (literally, "seven sisters road") was named after the tale of seven girls who took a vow of sisterhood. Ng Pa Ling (pen name of O Yeung Hak) describes the story in "The Legend of the Seven Sisters," from the first volume of his *Hong Kong Folktales*, as "magical as well as erotic." Once there were seven girls who were inseparable: they thought alike, they looked alike, and they loved one another dearly. They decided to make a vow to become sworn sisters and always "dress their own hair."

"Dress their own hair" refers to a widespread custom in the Shun Tak countryside in Guangdong. In those days, unmarried women wore their hair in a long plait, while married women wore theirs in a bun. On her wedding day, the bride's plait would be combed out and shaped into a bun by an elder relative; by adopting the term "dress their own hair," these young women indicated that since they had no intention of getting married, there was no need for anyone else to do their hair for them.

It came about that the third sister committed suicide by throwing herself into the sea in order to avoid an enforced marriage arranged by her parents. Honoring their pledge that "though not born on the same day, month, or year, they would die on the same day, month, and year," the remaining sisters also threw themselves into the sea. It is said that when their bodies were recovered, the sisters were holding one another's hands.

It was also said that their bodies were never found, and the next day a reef appeared at the place where they had drowned, resembling seven sisters holding hands and standing in a row from the tallest to the shortest. People called it Seven Sisters Reef. Later, when Seven Sisters Reef was buried in the mud following land reclamation, the new site was called Tsat Tsz Mui after the sisters, and it became a popular bathing spot in the early twentieth century. After a string of accidents in which male bathers were drowned, some rumormongers claimed that they were sacrificed to the spirits of the seven sisters. However, other people pointed out that the young women had already attained their ideal of pure sisterhood, and there was no reason for them to make trouble for the detested male sex.

Another version of the story was the diametrical opposite (although not without similarities). There were also seven sworn sisters in this version, but they had vowed to wed on the same day, month, and year. In the end, they managed to get married on the same day to seven brothers. On their wedding night, each of the sisters lay in bed with her new husband, performing the same ritual, when suddenly the third brother became enraged. Since his bride had failed to bleed, he was threatening to cast her out. Tormented by her husband's suspicions, accusations, and disgust, the unhappy young woman threw herself into the sea. The remaining six, resolutely abandoning their husbands, followed her dead body into the billows. In this version, Seven Sisters Reef on the coastline represents the seven brothers (including the third brother, overcome by remorse), who were turned into rock as they despairingly kept watch for their wives along the shore.

This version is recounted by the feminist scholar Chang Oi Ping in her *Rereading Hong Kong Legends*, published in 1993. Chang argues that the legend of the seven sisters was "neither erotic nor magical" but "a sorry and painful reflection of the social relationships between the two sexes in those days."

Tsat Tsz Mui Road, located between North Point and Quarry Bay in the northeastern part of Hong Kong Island, was constructed only after World War II and had seven haphazardly connected sections. The last two sections were separated by the Model Housing Estate, leaving the final section in a state of lonely desolation.

Archaeologists once attempted to excavate the reclamation area along Tsat Tsz Mui Road to uncover the original site where the Seven Sisters Reef was buried. Going on imprecise rumors, they worked out seven likely locations, including one under a roadside postbox and another under a florist's. Eventually they unearthed from the separate sites seven wooden combs, each with a long lock of hair entwined in it.

34

CANAL ROAD EAST AND CANAL ROAD WEST

Map readers have long felt perplexed about the existence of two parallel streets in Wan Chai on Hong Kong Island, one to the east and one to the west, both almost identical in length and breadth. But you only have to look at a map of Wan Chai from 1922 or earlier to understand why the street was divided into two down the middle. You will also learn why these twin streets running in the same direction are named for a canal although there is no canal in sight. (Their name in Cantonese is an approximation of the pronunciation of "canal").

Canal Road used to be the place where Wong Nai Chung, a mountain brook from a valley in the island's interior, flowed into the harbor. Local people called it Goose Brook because it was narrow and curved along this stretch. The fourth governor of Hong Kong, Sir John Bowring, converted the farmland in front of Wong Nai Chung Village into a racecourse (afterward known as Happy Valley) in 1857. He also built a canal by widening the surface of Goose Brook and raising the height of the bank, so people then called the waterway Bowring Canal. The parallel streets built on either side of the canal became Canal Road East and Canal Road West. The canal itself was covered over in the 1920s as part of the land-reclamation project taking place on the foreshores of Wan

Chai, after which no trace of the waterway was left above ground, apart from the two streets lined up together.

It was the fate of Canal Road East and Canal Road West (as with so many other places in Victoria) for a separation between sign and referent to take place in the course of successive stages of time and space. A more thorough deconstruction would be to take the argument one step further, that is, when the signifier for the sign "canal" no longer had a natural connection with its signified, then only the phonetic form remained in "canal," acting as a place-name, while the content of "canal" was abandoned. The underground waterway no longer existed in reality, no matter whether on a map or in people's comprehension. The street name not only made it impossible for anyone to trace its source, it actually tells us how the city deconstructs itself in its unceasing growth.

There used to be a wooden bridge at the intersection of the canal and Hennessy Road in those days; people called it Goose Neck Bridge, and the area around it was called Goose Neck District. A large number of banyan trees were planted along each side of the bridge, which led to it being designated one of the eight sights of Hong Kong with the name Goose Brook Banyan Grove, either because people used to cool down in the shade of the trees or because they went fishing along its banks.

Although the Western imagery of the goose that laid golden eggs has no counterpart in Chinese legend, "goose neck" is the name given to a strategically important narrow stretch of land or sea, and to cover over Goose Brook was tantamount to strangulation or beheading. After Goose Brook was buried underground, the local residents used to make sacrifices to the goose god outside the newly opened Goose Neck street market at Goose Neck Bridge. It was forbidden to sell roast goose at the street market, but on the fifteenth day of the lunar new year, a healthy live goose was selected for people to worship and then released afterward. If you set aside the superstitious nature of this activity and approach it from the perspective of cultural analysis, it is possible to see the goose worship as a positive (if illusory) strategy for preserving a link between a place and its name, not to mention a link between the name's signifier and signified.

From this point of view, it is not difficult to understand the custom of "beating the scoundrel," which it is said became popular afterward at Goose Neck Bridge without a goose neck bridge and Canal Road without a canal. In a city where a place, its name, and its meaning move inexorably toward dissolution, it is inevitable that a counterpolicy of reconstructing meaning will be implemented. That is, a completely unrelated sign (paper figures used in "beating the scoundrel") becomes through a kind of wishful thinking the actual referent (the real-life target in "beating the scoundrel" is usually a person who provokes disgust or hatred). Further, people obtain acute psychological relief and comfort in the course of this fictitious representation (the action of repeatedly and violently beating the paper scoundrel with a shoe, usually supplemented with vicious cursing).

It is therefore no accident that beating the scoundrel takes place under Goose Neck Bridge. The premise underlying the practice of beating the scoundrel is that the person thus represented is in reality beyond our grasp, so that its efficacy is operative only in a place where the referents are lost, and its result is by the same token destined to be ineffective.

35

ALDRICH STREET

Aldrich Street was situated in Shau Kei Wan in the northeastern part of Hong Kong Island. It was named after a section of the harbor called Aldrich Bay, since one end of the street went up to the waterfront. There also used to be an Aldrich Village on the hillside at the other end of the street.

Aldrich Bay itself was named after Major Aldrich, who after signing the Treaty of Nanjing in 1842 was sent to Hong Kong by military headquarters, charged with the task of drawing up a detailed plan for stationing a British garrison in Hong Kong. Major Aldrich devised a grandiose scheme that included a military cantonment occupying spacious grounds in a marvelously symmetrical design as well as an impregnable defense strategy. The cantonment was to cover the area of what afterward became Admiralty Barracks, Central District, Government Hill, and the Botanic Gardens. In Aldrich's imagination, this huge invincible fortress would become the center and symbol of Hong Kong Island. However, the governor at that time, Sir Henry Pottinger, firmly opposed Aldrich's plans and insisted that Central be reserved for commercial purposes. In the end, Major Aldrich's dream of a military city was never realized.

Major Aldrich's main contribution to Hong Kong, it was said, lay instead in overhauling army discipline. Morale among the soldiers was low, in part because the British forces failed to adjust to the environment in those early years and malaria was rife. It did not help that the men were generally of low character, who regarded looting and pillaging in occupied territory as a normal occupation, while drunkenness and brawls were common. Major Aldrich transferred soldiers who committed disciplinary offenses from the urban area to A Kung Ngam, a remote outpost that afterward became the Lei Yue Mun Battery. The new regulations and severe penalties he also introduced eventually brought the soldiers under control. Presumably to commemorate Major Aldrich's achievements, the government named the bay at Shau Kei Wan after him, and the name Aldrich Bay appears on the map of Hong Kong drawn up by Lieutenant Collinson in 1845. The characters chosen to represent the major's name in Chinese, which translate literally as "cherish order," are highly appropriate.

Major Aldrich observed a stringent self-discipline in his personal life, down to the details of his daily routine. For example, even under heavy fire on the field of battle he still insisted on taking afternoon tea every day at four o'clock. His manner of speaking was very precise and carefully articulated, and he never permitted anyone to interrupt him. In some respects the major could be considered an antimilitarist, because his fierce detestation of chaos was such that he could not tolerate the disorder of war, which left dead bodies strewn everywhere.

It is not known when the apotheosis of Major Aldrich took place. It could have been at a fairly early stage when local villagers were subjected to repeated pirate raids. Major Aldrich's zealousness in stationing massive numbers of troops on garrison duty protected the security of the area, with the result that villagers regarded him as a godlike figure to whom they could pray for peace. As the story was passed down from generation to generation, Aldrich became mantled in mystery. Eventually some people built a temple consecrated to Aldrich along the foreshore to make offerings to "Lord" Aldrich (whose image was impressive enough to rival the ancient warrior-hero General Kwan), and it became as splendid as the nearby Tam Kung Temple at A Kung Ngam. It was said that the spirit of Aldrich appeared several times at the height of the rioting over the Star Ferry fare increase in 1966, admonishing people to obey the Royal Hong Kong Police Force.

Aldrich Bay has disappeared from 1997 Hong Kong street maps as a result of land reclamation, and nothing remains of Aldrich Temple or Aldrich Village.

POSSESSION STREET

There is an extra layer of meaning to the name of Possession Street that is usually concealed by its historical significance. Its English name comes from Possession Point, where the British occupying forces first landed on Hong Kong Island's northwestern shore. Local people called it Shui Hang Hau (literally, "the mouth of a water course"), marking the spot where a stream flowed down the hill and into the harbor.

In January 1841, following the First Opium War, while Captain Charles Elliot, the British plenipotentiary and superintendent of trade, was negotiating the Convention of Chuanbi with Qishan, the Qing emperor's personal representative, the British man-of-war *Sulphur* went ahead and occupied Hong Kong Island. Its captain, Edward Belcher, has given the following account in his *Narrative of a Voyage round the World Performed in HMS Sulphur*:

> We landed on Monday, the 25th, at fifteen minutes past eight, and being the bona fide first possessors, Her Majesty's health was drank with three cheers on Possession Mount. On the 26th the squadron arrived; the marines were landed, the union hoisted on our post, and formal possession taken of the island, by Commodore Sir J. G. Bremer, accompanied

by the other officers of the squadron, under a feu-de-joie from the marines, and a royal salute from the ships of war.

At the beginning of the Royal Navy's occupation, when the British troops were stationed at Possession Point, their quarters were no more than a collection of tents and mat-sheds. The area became known in Chinese as Sai Ying Pun (literally, "Western barracks") and in English as West Point. A combination of poor sanitation and difficulties in acclimatization led to an epidemic of fever with a very high death rate, and a state of panic set in. A rumor even began to circulate that the local inhabitants had laid a curse on the water supply. This rumor subsided after the barracks were moved to an area east of Central, but the curse lingered. As the city developed, a stretch of open ground near Possession Street, popularly known as Tai Tat Tei (literally, "large bamboo-mat ground"), was taken over by all kinds of riffraff, from entertainers to herbal doctors and fortune-tellers. One of the latter, who called himself Spiritual Diviner, proclaimed that the fung shui was detrimental to the British. The British, for their part, also kept their distance from this disreputable native quarter.

In the early days, the Chinese name for Possession Street was a phonetic transcription of its English name. As it happens, the word "possession," apart from meaning ownership or control, also has the meaning of being possessed by spirits, or madness. The Chinese name was eventually changed to Shui Hang Hau, and it became the haunt of Chinese high-class courtesans before the government moved the brothels to Shek Tong Tsui in 1903. A government sanitation officer by the name of J. A. Davidson defied the foreigners' taboo on this area; forsaking the red-light district for Westerners in Lyndhurst Terrace in Central, he would visit the Chinese brothels in Shui Hang Hau, where he fell madly in love with a local prostitute named Butterfly. One day, after a night of passion (and in the grip of a hangover), he lost his footing on the embankment, fell into the harbor, and drowned. It is said that his demise was caused by his "possession" by the spirit of Butterfly's late father.

Professor S. Clark, who taught in the Department of History at the University of Hong Kong prior to World War II and was also a student of Chinese fortune-telling in his spare time, maintained in his *The ABCs of Chinese Fortune-Telling and Its Application to Hong Kong* that the English word "possession" was highly inauspicious. He proposed changing the name to Exorcism Street in order to restore good fung shui. The Chinese equivalent of "exorcism" is *gon gwai*, literally meaning "expelling ghosts" or "expelling devils"; it is not known if Clark was aware that foreigners are referred to colloquially in Chinese as "foreign devils."

37

SYCAMORE STREET

Sycamore Street is located in Tai Kok Tsui on the Kowloon Peninsula. On the map it looks like a bow, with Maple Street intersecting
it at the center of its curve, and another, smaller bow-shaped street,
Willow Street, running parallel with it.

There are several different stories about the name of this street.
The generally accepted explanation is that the street was originally
given its English name that was then transposed into Chinese as
Si-go-mo Gai (literally, "poetry, song, and dance street"). It is said
that when Tai Kok Tsui first underwent development, the authori-
ties decided to name the newly built streets after trees, so that
Pine Street, Oak Street, Beech Street, Elm Street, Ivy Street, Cherry
Street, Maple Street, Willow Street, Poplar Street, Cedar Street, and
so on all appear in this area. These streets were originally named in
English and their names were then translated into Chinese. Syca-
more Street should have been no exception. Yet why is Sycamore
Street rendered phonetically rather than according to its meaning?

One explanation that has a certain persuasive force is that the
sycamore was taken to be a kind of fig tree known in Chinese as
mou-fa-gwo, which literally means "lacking flowers or fruit." However, Tai Kok Tsui had a population of local people with a firm belief
in the magical properties of names. Since the words "lacking flowers or fruit" are diametrically opposite to the traditional Chinese

well-wisher's greeting for "blooming flowers and plentiful fruit," the name of the street was transposed phonetically out of respect for the local culture. The words "poetry," "song," and "dance" are not only very fine in themselves but strung together also have the associated meaning of putting on a show to celebrate peace and prosperity.

However, there is an alternative explanation (assuming that the English name is the original one), since it is by no means certain exactly what kind of tree the sycamore is. In Europe it is a large kind of maple, but in America it is a plane tree, and in the eastern Mediterranean region it refers to a fig tree. There is no obvious reason why sycamore has to be translated as *mou-fa-gwo*. Perhaps it is just that the official translators at the time had no way of selecting which meaning of sycamore to translate so chose instead to transcribe the word phonetically.

Another account (not terribly convincing but one that people preferred to believe) circulated widely among local people. Leung Kwan Yat recorded the story in his *A Study of the Oral History of the Kowloon Area*. As far back as the eighteenth century, the stretch of land that became Poetry, Song, and Dance Street was already a center of artistic, educational, and cultural activities for the whole district thanks to its proximity to Mong Kok, one of the largest villages in Kowloon. Ancestral temples, schools, and opera troupes served the community's religious, educational, and leisure needs. In time a scholar from Mong Kok bestowed on it the name Poetry, Song, and Dance, after a well-known passage in the preface to the ancient *Book of Poetry*:

> Poetry is where intention goes. In one's heart, it is intention; in words it becomes poetry. When feelings stir within, they are formed into words. When words are not enough, so there

are sighs; when sighs are not enough, so they take form in song; and when song is not enough, so, without thought, hands and feet dance.

Poetry, Song, and Dance had declined by the beginning of the twentieth century, along with Mong Kok's decline and disappearance as a village. Instead it degenerated into a zone of brothels and whores with noisy entertainment night after night. When the British developed Tai Kok Tsui, they named the street Sycamore after the pronunciation of the old name of the area, Si-go-mo, an act that showed disrespect for Chinese tradition and indifference to local culture and custom.

Some people have uncovered evidence to suggest that this stretch of land had been planted with fig trees, uprooted when the street was under construction. It was subsequently named Sycamore Street in English, while its Chinese name was adopted for the sake of its secondary association with peace and prosperity. Later the government replanted the street with bauhinia, the city's emblematic flower, in order to enhance the street's scenic attractions. A large number of schools were established along the street during the second half of the twentieth century, reviving the tradition of poetry, song, and dance.

Although the fig tree has no flowers, it bears fruit; the bauhinia has flowers but it is barren.

TUNG CHOI STREET AND SAI YEUNG CHOI STREET

Tung Choi Street (literally, "water spinach street") and Sai Yeung Choi Street (watercress street) were a pair of streets of roughly equal length running side by side north to south in Mong Kok. This state of affairs, however, was a relatively late development. Tung Choi Street and Sai Yeung Choi Street actually underwent three separate stages of development, but the first two stages have almost been forgotten. The unusual relationship between the two streets allows us a glimpse of how the intrinsic quality of a place can stubbornly persist, overriding superficial changes. It also gives us an understanding of what is called the spirit of a place in Chinese culture, a variant of naturist mysticism.

According to Leung To's *The Origins of Kowloon Street Names*, the middle section of what became Tung Choi Street and Sai Yeung Choi Street used to be a stretch of paddy fields in Mong Kok Village. As it happens, water spinach (*tung-choi*) has low resistance to the cold and is therefore grown in the summer, while watercress (*sai-yeung-choi*) is just the opposite, so that the farmers in Mong Kok at the time practiced a form of crop rotation, growing water spinach in the paddies in summer and planting watercress at the end of autumn. Afterward, when the Mong Kok paddy fields were filled in and leveled in the course of the area's redevelopment, two new roads that were built there were named Tung Choi Street and Sai Yeung Choi Street.

However, before Tung Choi Street and Sai Yeung Choi Street became two separate streets, they had in fact been one. This was the first stage in the relationship between the two streets. In the initial stage of the street's construction, it was no more than a muddy path, lined with new low-roofed huts built to house Mong Kok's original inhabitants. Following their long-established custom of rotating between water spinach and watercress, the inhabitants called the street Tung Choi Street in the summertime and changed it to Sai Yeung Choi Street on the arrival of winter. In consequence, if you look up early administrative and post office records, you will find that the address of this street is sometimes given as Tung Choi Street and sometimes as Sai Yeung Choi Street, depending on the season when the forms were filled in. If you sent a letter to Tung Choi Street in the summertime but wrote the name Sai Yeung Choi Street by mistake, it might be winter before it got delivered. This, of course, was something of a nuisance to the inhabitants, but they still maintained their simple, uncomplaining nature characteristic of village people, content and happy in their accustomed ways.

Nevertheless, the situation described above was quite inconvenient as far as local government departments were concerned, and the authorities decided to redevelop the district, creating two separate roads, Tung Choi Street and Sai Yeung Choi Street, in order to avoid further confusion. But the inhabitants did not give way so easily. Obedient to the timetable of alternating seasons so deeply implanted in their being, the whole populace, without a word being spoken, shifted over to Tung Choi Street and conducted their trade there for the summer, and then in winter they moved their places of residence and work back to Sai Yeung Choi Street, so that each street would be in turn deserted for one half of the year. The post might still be delivered up to six months late, and the local government and administration both found it difficult to impose uniformity.

Although the problem was a matter of great frustration to the government, Time itself proved to be the best solution. As the next generation grew up and flourished in the two streets and the older generation gradually died out, the mode of existence based on the two rotating seasons eventually decayed as well. In addition, the government set about moving outsiders into the district and encouraging the original inhabitants to move out, effectively destroying what was left of the solidarity and unique sense of identity within the village. The third stage was in fact a poststructural state of the dissolution of spatial-temporal differences, the breakdown of the winter/summer binary opposition, and the obliteration of the distinction between water spinach and watercress. Young career women shopping for vegetables in the street market would mistake watercress for water spinach and vice versa. The problem was that their husbands never noticed that there was anything odd about it as they gulped it down.

39

SAI YEE STREET

Sai Yee Street (literally, "laundry street") in Mong Kok used to be a stream in the days before Mong Kok Village became urbanized. From its source in Beacon Hill to the north, its water was used to irrigate the nearby flower nurseries and vegetable gardens. In the 1920s, when the paddy fields of Mong Kok were leveled and the area was developed into a residential district, it was the custom of the inhabitants to wash their clothes and lay them out to dry at the side of the stream. Doing the laundry gradually became a specialized occupation, and many local women made a living out of it. It was at this point that the path along the bank became known as Sai Yee Street. Afterward the stream was covered over, when the city drew up new plans, but the new street that was built over the underground stream kept the old name.

People engaged in comparative cultural studies have made some research on the role played by Sai Yee Street in local culture. In his *Street Names and Indigenous Values*, for example, Ma Hak-ming attempted to interpret this kind of district culture with "laundry" as a signifier. Ma's argument was centered on the explanatory possibility of "water" in activities revolving around "laundry," in contrast to "fire," another element in everyday cultural practices. His main points are set out below.

First, the function of water in an activity such as laundry is not nourishment or the sustenance of life but a medium for washing, and the water used in the process of washing necessarily ends up depleted and is drained away. This is the opposite to water being used for drinking and irrigation. In terms of structural function, water used in laundry is totally different from fire used in cooking. That is, cooking transforms a substance so that it becomes capable of being ingested, while laundry brings about a substance's reversion to its former appearance, but the illusory longing for reversion is destined never to be truly satisfied (even if clothes are washed clean they can never again be the clothes before they were washed). To take laundry as a signifier of a district culture suggests a desire for self-preservation in the collective unconsciousness, and also the impossibility of this self-preservation.

Two, depletion in washing is unavoidably realized through rubbing, kneading, and beating. It is not the same as the destructiveness of cooking with fire, because washing in water does not induce an acute transformation but only creates a gradual and imperceptible erosion. It could also be said that if the violence of fire is carried out without any sense of shame in public, then water's violence is protracted and hidden, with the sensual effects of clearing, cooling, and cleansing.

Three, it is difficult in laundry culture to transcend the contradictions inherent in its nature. The aim of laundering is to achieve purity but its inevitable result is pollution. Clean river water becomes dirty water, and the consciousness ends in confusion. Unlike refining through fire, which produces an internal transformation, laundering must make an external and temporary restoration through the annulment of its own medium (water). Laundry culture, at the same time as it is intent on cleansing itself, also necessarily brings about the soiling of the Other; or, to put it another way, the brightness and cleanliness of what has been washed are achieved at the cost of the filthiness of the means of washing.

Four, apart from the illusion of reversion in washing, laundry also emphasizes the function of clothes in covering and adorning. We can imagine how the culture of dish washing realistically reflects the way of life of people who earn a living, whereas laundry is aimed at the temporary undressing and repeated cleaning of collective civilization's outer garments. Although laundry culture is essentially an attribute of lower-class working women, when it ascends to symbolize a district's specific character, it must at the same time reveal a general and intrinsic meaning that structuralist anthropology cannot ignore.

40

PUBLIC SQUARE STREET

Yau Ma Tei's Public Square Street is now called Jung-fong Gai (literally, "people's quarter street") in Cantonese, but before the 1970s it was known as Gung-jung Sei-fong Gai (public square street, that is, "square" as in an equal-sided rectangle). Some commentators have said that *gung-jung sei-fong* was a mistranslation of the English term "public square" and that the correct translation should have been Gung-jung Gwong-cheung (literally, "public plaza"). The name in English referred to an empty space in the street popularly known as Banyan Head. Itinerant performers would gather there at nightfall, casting divinations and telling fortunes, or singing and storytelling. Afterward, when street names were being revised, it was called People's Quarter Street in Cantonese, taking on the meaning of a space where the populace at large would gather.

However, some people believe that *gung-jung sei-fong* was not a mistranslation but was based on fact. Before the Kowloon Peninsula was ceded to Britain in 1860, there was a square plaza at this spot for the use of the people of the neighborhood as a meeting place and market. Running around the plaza was a street in the shape of a square. This street did not have a beginning nor did it have an end, instead turning back in on itself. In addition, the four sides were of equal length, and the corners were at a uniform angle. The buildings along both sides of any one of these four streets were perfect matches for the buildings on the other three sides, whether in height, design, or order. The faces of the street's inhabitants were also difficult to distinguish one from another, and strangers passing through could even less count on determining where they were by looking at the clothing hung out to dry from the upper stories. To enter the square street was to enter an absolutely predictable and calculable geometrical world, where there was only a single length and a single angle. However, it was actually the square street's regular and monotonous construction that made it a labyrinth from which it was difficult to escape. In fact, a square street, wholly self-contained and with a name matching reality, has neither entrance nor exit. Therefore, the plaza enclosed by the square street was a sealed plaza, and the public nature of the street made it at the same time a private one.

The only way of finding one's way in the square street seems to have been by determining the direction. The four sides of the square street were fixed according to the four points of the compass, north, south, east, and west, but because there were no door numbers along the street (for no one could say where the street began and where it ended), it was rather difficult to determine if one were proceeding along the east street, the west street, the north street, or the south street. To be sure, this was not a problem for the local inhabitants, because whatever side of the street they lived on made no difference to them. Another special characteristic of the square street was that there was a flight of steps at each corner. It was said that if you kept turning right as you walked, the steps would lead upward, but if you went in the opposite direction, to the left, the steps would lead down. But whether you went up or down, you would still return to your original place by way of the four flights of steps and the four corners. Experts in cartography maintain that such phenomena can occur only on the surface of maps, or in pictures with fanciful optical illusions.

The conclusion of some map archaeologists was that Public Square Street was previously a walled village in the shape of a square, and what is known as the plaza was in fact an empty space at the center of the village. After 1860, new streets were laid out in Kowloon, and Public Square Street lost its original appearance when the village wall was torn down.

Adherents of the psychoanalytic school of cartography maintain that the inhabitants of Public Square Street suffered from the combined afflictions of agoraphobia and claustrophobia. There is also a contrary view to the effect that these two diseases could not exist at all in the world of Public Square Street.

4-1

CEDAR STREET

It would be a mistake to believe that street names are loquacious by nature. If you open a street directory of any city in the past you will discover that the great majority of streets are silent. Such is the case with Cedar Street, a street that is hardly worth mentioning. On the map it was just a side street located between Sham Shui Po and Mong Kok in Kowloon. There was nothing about it that distinguished it among the streets in the vicinity that are named after trees. It had nothing outstanding of its own, nor did it represent anything that would win the affections of a tourist guide or local poet; it did not have a role to play in the history of this city, leaving a mark behind it. It did not even have an opportunity to appear in a street anecdote or rumor. It was just the kind of street with nothing about it that could attract the interest of map readers.

The only place where we could find a passage describing Cedar Street is in a book about maps. Its author was a minor writer of the late twentieth century who grew up and began to write in Cedar Street. In this unsystematic and unclassifiable collection of map reading, and with a complete disregard for reality, the author read in between the dotted lines and colored spots strewn freely across the page all sorts of public and private nightmares, memories, longings, and speculations. His account of Cedar Street is as follows:

I have long contemplated the impossibility of returning to Cedar Street. With only a street map before me, how can I summon up once more the image of Cedar Street from the depths of my memory simply by fixing my eyes on this tiny, brown, slanting patch with its surroundings and text on the map? How should I find the scent of cedar on the map, or hear the sound of the wind in its branches? And how should my fingers trace the tree trunks' rough pattern on the map's smooth surface? Why is there no map to reproduce its sound, its feel, its scent? Why is it not possible for us to seize the surface appearance of things, their most impermanent feature, and in so doing to penetrate their essence? But I can only recall another map, a map of my own home environment that I showed off to my schoolmates when I was a child; sketched by an inexperienced hand, it showed a shady road densely planted with cedars and a few spacious low houses standing widely apart. I even drew a fictional sheepdog into that nonexistent courtyard. Afterward, this sketch gradually disappeared under the superimposition of the street plan based on an actual survey, and in the end all that remained was a short, narrow section surrounded by names like Portland Street, Ki Lung Street, Tai Nan Street, and Yu Chau Street, with their connotations of the most banal and vulgar aspects of life. However, it is precisely in this kind of urban area that I construct the dwelling place of my memory, allowing my words to soar upward, take root downward, and branch out inquiringly and playfully in an image of a cedar.

In a South American myth, the cedar tree is a treasure chest full of words. People are supposed to make an opening in its trunk and listen to the words concealed inside it. Those who can hear them will find the place where they belong; those who cannot hear them will drift like dust in the breeze.

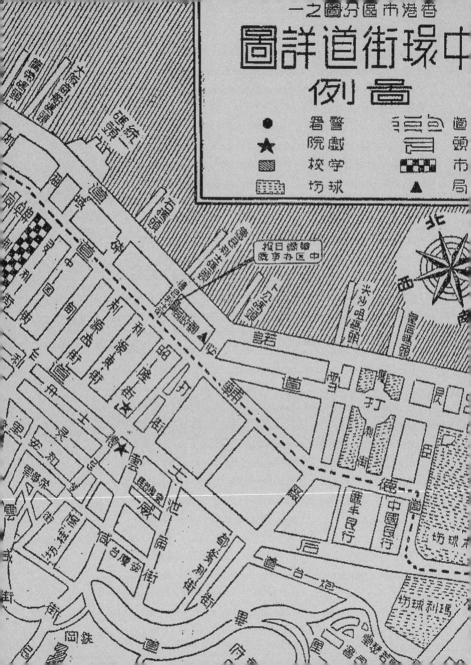

香港市區分圖之一

中環街道詳圖

圖 例

●	警署			道頭
★	戲院			市局
▨	學校		▦	
	球坊		▲	

北

中區辦事處
華標日報

PART FOUR

Signs

42

THE DECLINE OF THE LEGEND

In China, one of the earliest maps to use legends systematically is the Ming dynasty "Grand World Map," published by Luo Hongxian (1504–1564) in 1555. The "Grand World Map" was Luo Hongxian's revised and enlarged version of the Yuan magnum opus "World Map" by Zhu Siben (1273–1337). Its legend divides urban areas into three levels, using white squares to show cities at the prefectural level, white lozenges for the district level, and white circles for the county level. It also uses white triangles for military post stations and black squares for transport stations and so on. In addition, units such as state farms, forts, walled cities, defiles, regimental camps, postal relay stations, frontier passes, border garrisons, beacon mounds, terraces, pacification offices, pacification commissions, military commissions, and chieftain's offices are distinguished by geometrical signs of different shapes. Setting up legends like these allowed a range of distinctions, lacking in the earlier version, to be made for significant features of the landscape. You could even say that legend signs enriched the vocabulary of maps and made their grammar more complex. Legends are the inevitable product of a constant development in map language.

Nevertheless, it would be inadvisable to regard legends as a purely passive outcome in the history of cartography. In fact, the appearance of legends automatically transformed the basic character of maps, adding a narrative aspect to the pictorial aspect. The modern use of the word "legend" includes all explanatory wording in images, maps, and illustrations. Therefore a legend is a place where images and writing converge and interact, a glossary of two languages. As a script it gives a semantic structure to qualitative or quantitative signs that are basically without an inherent meaning: for instance, the relationship between the three levels of prefectural, district, and county cities, allowing the juxtaposition of synchronic signs to produce a diachronic narrative connection, such as outlining the potentiality of itineraries along navigable rivers or passable roads. In the end, legends allow maps to tell stories.

We can imagine what kind of legends tell what kind of stories. Legends about walled cities, border forts, and garrisons tell a story of military attacks and defense; legends about post stations, roads, and circuits tell stories of mothers parted from sons and husbands from wives; legends about ports, shipping lanes, and blue water tell stories of danger, conquests, and roaming. The design of representational signs in legends observes the principle of generalization; the requirement of symbolization conversely belongs to a secondary category, because the nature of signs is by no means mimetic but indicative. Therefore the relationship between signs and writing is arbitrary, and conversion from one to the other is extremely flexible. In theory, legends conceal a huge imaginative range; we can use any kind of sign to show a written concept, and we can use any kind of method, simple or complicated, to divide or unify the geographical elements to be expressed, or use any kind of image, whether close or distant, to weave together the semantic and syntactic morphemes. Different ways of using legends can turn a map into open-ended polysemic fiction offering innumerable stories: amazing and anodyne, happy and tragic, tracing routes from south to north and west to east, traversing longitudes and latitudes, winding around hills and rivers, following post roads and railways, crossing fields and deserts, passing mountains and lakes, and penetrating forests and valleys.

However, as legends developed, not only did they fail to expand the possibility of signs as a form of language; on the contrary, they turned into a limitation. To serve their instrumental purpose more efficiently, legends became uniform, compulsory supplements without any imaginative power to speak of. The language of maps became rigid. There was nothing in existence more arid than maps, which were reduced to games in the exercise of power, whether in regard to knowledge, economics, or politics. It is only when individual ways of reading legends return that we can again read legends as tales of marvels.

43

THE EYE OF THE TYPHOON

"Hong Kong Buying from the World," published by the Hong Kong Survey and Mapping Office in 1987, generated a fairly intense dispute among economist and climatologist map readers. It is a world map of the five continents, whose most prominent feature is its broad arrow lines that stretch from every country across the world, pointing in beautiful shades of purple toward an all but invisible city off the coast of the South China Sea. These complex arrows are vectors indicating by means of gradations in width and hue the quality and direction of the flow of commodities. The tail of the arrow from Europe, for example, is divided into seven sections, like streamers at the end of a banner, or the tail feathers of a cock pheasant; the lines from Africa, India, Australia, and Southeast Asia are like flames from an explosion flaring in all directions, or like a hundred rivers converging; the lines from South and North America are like the long tongues of snakes or lizards; the line from Japan sweeps down like a gale-force wind; the line from mainland China is like a gigantic finger pressing on the island's head. A box in the upper-left corner explains that it is a pictorial record of Hong Kong's imports from abroad in the period January to December 1985; the total value of the goods, given in billions of Hong Kong dollars, is printed at the top of each arrowhead. For instance, the figure 28.9 appears beside the arrow from Europe, 24.6 beside the arrow from the Americas, 53.3 from Japan, and 59 from mainland China. Tables in the lower half give breakdowns of imports according to transportation routes, the increase in the value of imports from each major country within the last decade, and the value of each category of goods and its growth.

From the economists' point of view, this map constructs a pattern of local economic existence indexed by imports, setting out the broad outlines of Hong Kong's import activities (without losing the details) by utilizing a rich and abundant range of images (such as graphs of arrowheads and means of transport), and a number of visually informative tables (such as three-dimensional pie charts and column charts). It could also be said that although falling short of truly scientific cartography in terms of its basic construction and value, this map still matches up to highly precise geomorphologic maps with respect to its location's material existence. In a certain sense, it even surpasses large-scale survey maps, because it can capture the actual physiognomy of the location without recourse to drawing an image of it; compared with the actual earth's surface at that location, it can abstract a more material essence and dispense with the need for any depiction of the location itself. It is even impossible to draw the location itself, because in a small-scale map (i.e., a microscopic version of the macrocosm), this location actually lacks the plasticity of cartography. To expand into a world-shaking cyclone, forcing the projection of its own image on the global stage, this location is wholly dependent on the value that it absorbs—value in the literal sense. It then becomes the equivalent to what it has absorbed, neither more nor less.

Specialist climatologists reading this map, however, had a completely different way of looking at it. They believed that this map depicts a large-scale global climate change in 1985, together with the major typhoon that was caused by this change. High pressure over the five continents had the effect that air currents happened to converge over this small island off the coast of the South China Sea, forming a violent cyclone across the whole island. According to the records, this global cyclone strengthened without abating over the next ten years and showed signs of persistent duration. As the force of the cyclone increased so did the destruction it created in equal measure. There was calm at the heart of the cyclone, however, because it was empty.

Semiologist map readers, adopting the climatologists' analysis, concluded that this map explains the islanders' field of vision.

44

~

CHEK LAP KOK AIRPORT

The secret of the Chek Lap Kok Airport plan is now beyond the reach of anyone to uncover. The only clue that remains to us is a blueprint drawn up in 1990 of Hong Kong's seaport and airport development, called "Construction for the Future." This blueprint, which displays the development of port facilities in Hong Kong at the end of the twentieth century, includes sea-lane plans, container wharves expansion, and harbor reclamation projects. It also outlines the so-called new airport plan in documents and records, that is, the enormous concept that begins with the new Chek Lap Kok location of the airport on the north shore of Lantao Island and includes a range of developments such as the airport railway and residential, industrial, and commercial sites along the shoreline. It is worth pointing out that this blueprint emphasizes the importance of Hong Kong as a seaport and airport, by hinting at its two possible exits—by sea and by air.

Some people think, however, that the section on seaport construction in this "Construction for the Future" blueprint was only camouflage, its main purpose being a strategy for airport development. What was the ultimate point of this strategy? The superficial explanation is that the old Kai Tak Airport in the city center was already bursting at the seams, and since it had no way of meeting the needs of the city's continuously expanding volume of air traffic, the only option was to build a new international airport. However, to the sharp eyes of scholars of strategic cartography, there was an ulterior scheme behind the construction of a new airport: what was being planned was by no means an airport in the traditional sense but a mobile airport. Their guess was that the plan for the airport was at the heart of an emergency contingency strategy. The point of this strategy was to cope with major catastrophes such as nuclear accidents, earthquakes, epidemics, or alien invasions. The original concept was to separate a section of the surface of Hong Kong Island from the earth's crust and install a huge propeller on it, converting it into a mobile port, but this plan was later abandoned because the size of the project made it unfeasible. Mobility had all along been the central concept in the contingency strategy, because in a city that lacked the ability to defend itself in every respect, escape was the only way out in the event of disaster.

Where the airport in question was constructed on new land reclaimed from the harbor, the prospect of mobility was obviously quite close to reality. The expression "airport" actually means "a port in the air." The "Construction for the Future" blueprint had a drawing next to the site of the airport at Chek Lap Kok of a three-dimensional schematic diagram of an airport rising to a flight path in the sky. In the lower left-hand corner of the map was a predicative table, showing that the capacity of the airport could reach forty million passengers by 2008, that is, six times the population of the territory. Given ideal conditions in the railway transportation system from the city to the airport, it was estimated that the total population could reach Chek Lap Kok airport in safety within three hours of an incident taking place and be aboard the airport after a further two hours as it moved away from the mainland. The airport's flight and landing technology, its range and speed, and conflicts related to its movement in regard to airspace, land borders, and territorial waters were details that are so far unknown. No one even knows whether or not the airport in the end ever actually became airborne.

45

THE METONYMIC SPECTRUM

Reading a map of land use in Hong Kong drawn up in 1987 can help us gain a deeper understanding of the metonymic possibilities allowed by color distribution. From the explanation given in the map legend, we learn that the separate land uses represented by different colors were as follows: red for commercial districts; orange for public housing estates; dark brown for high-density residential districts; light brown for low-density residential districts; purple for industrial districts; blue for government and communal public facilities (including schools, hospitals, and communications facilities); green for entertainment and recreational areas; yellow for cemeteries and crematoria; white for vacant land or areas under development. On this map, red is concentrated mainly in the area bordered by Nathan Road from Mong Kok to Tsim Sha Tsui in the Kowloon Peninsula and Central District in Hong Kong Island; there is a scattering of orange in the northern part of the Kowloon Peninsula; dark brown occupies the widest swath, spreading all over Kowloon and the north shore of Hong Kong Island; concentrations of light brown can be found only at Kowloon Tong in the north of Kowloon, along with the Peak and Jardine's Lookout on Hong Kong Island; purple patches are rather few, scattered around the Cheung Sha Wan and Tai Kok Tsui in West Kowloon and San Po Kong and Kwun Tong in East Kowloon, along with Quarry Bay in the eastern district of Hong Kong Island; blue is particularly striking, occupying key locations in every district; green is dotted sparsely among them; yellow occurs in isolated patches along the northern boundaries of urban Kowloon and in Happy Valley on the southern edge of Hong Kong Island's urban area; white is mainly along the constantly changing shorelines.

In land-use maps we see the formation of a city's genealogy. One aspect of color differentiation is that it gives prominence to shifts in usage, but at the same time it emphasizes a kind of nonexistent and highly generalized, simplified, and purified division. Also, colors do not have any necessary intrinsic significance. Meaning can be shown by a color through its difference from other colors, and associated meanings can be conveyed by different densities or shades of the same color. Thus, just as orange turns into red, red becomes purple, purple becomes blue, blue becomes green, and green becomes yellow in a repeating cycle, the city through color both diverges and converges, separates and joins, is different and the same. (This is apart from the blank spaces without color.)

Nevertheless, the color spectrum does not actually have an independent existence; when the seven colors are overlaid, does it not amount to an apparently nonexistent white? If this is the case, white is the agglomeration of all colors, nothingness is the accumulation of things, and uselessness is the basis and ultimate end of usefulness. Further, if color is an aspect of appearance, we should be able to read other senses as well. Take hearing: red is a declaration of love; orange is the scream of a rape victim; dark brown is a sentimental announcement by the host on a TV show with on-the-spot reporting; light brown is belching, snoring, or barking; purple is the expiring moment of machinery in operation; blue is the MTR's "Please stand behind the yellow line" announcement; green is a furtive whisper; yellow is a mobile phone that no one answers; white is the sound of nature. This would be how color constructs a map of a city's sound zones. Or take smells: red is bacteria in a central air-conditioning system; orange is severed limbs in a refrigerator; dark brown is toilet disinfectant in the neighbors' bathroom; light brown is fermenting grapes in backyard dust bins; purple is congealed grease and sweat; blue is moldy wooden tables and chairs in government offices; green is the body odor of a young woman dressed in fashionable brand-name clothes; yellow is the twice-a-year scent of graveside flowers and dense smoke from hillside fires; white is pure dust. This would be how color constructs a map of urban odor zones. In principle, no matter what kind of imagery you invent in which the part stands for the whole, you can rationalize it through the design of a map legend.

In the distribution of similar colors, the combination of these three factors (usage, sound, and smell) creates several layers of metonyms, constituting another framework spectrum/genealogy: from matter to sense organs to states of mind. From this it is not hard to imagine a map of urban moods, recording the symptoms of a city's collective schizophrenia (such as hypocrisy, frenzy, apathy, disgust, boredom, submissiveness, restlessness, insomnia, and amnesia), and assembling patches of red, orange, dark brown, light brown, purple, blue, green, yellow, and white to compose a flourishing cityscape of dazzling diversity. What a map that is so rich in sensory stimulation requires is a way of reading the senses. This taking a part for the whole is a necessity for metonym, the basic nature of senses, and the stirring of desire.

46

~

THE ELEVATION OF IMAGINATION

From the development of elevation topography in the Hong Kong region, we can understand clearly how a place might not be willing to accept the limitations of flat surfaces, pulling away from the mediocrity that cannot permit height. What is meant by elevation is the vertical distance along a vertical line from the standard level of the earth, also known as height above sea level or true height; and what is meant by that level is the mean sea level. In other words, elevation means transcending the level.

Prior to the map in the 1819 *San-on County Gazetteer*, the maps of the Hong Kong region produced in China still adopted the method of panoramic landscape maps, in which height is shown by a hill-shaped schematic image. On the one hand, this highly symbolic method is easy for people who are familiar with this pictorial tradition to interpret; on the other hand, it is a complete submission to the fact that maps are flat, pressing what is seen from the side as a three-dimensional hill shape into a flat surface as seen from above looking down. It could also be said that the hill shapes in the landscape method are only generalized qualitative signs and not quantitative signs calculated on the basis of actual data; they could even be called the shape of hills but not their reality. The mood invoked by this kind of map is dignified with fine-sounding epithets such as "secluded elegance," but in reality it is more a matter of lethargy and indolence, lacking the will to emerge beyond secondary space.

Later, the nautical chart of Hong Kong drawn up by Captain Belcher in 1841 adopted the "landform hatching" method, which shows changes in gradient by means of hatches of different degrees of fineness and length together with unevenly placed blank patches, according to the shading of light rays cast on the earth's surface. Just as a sketch creates a three-dimensional space on paper with different shades of gray and varying line densities, this method of hatching makes for the first time the topography appear like a detailed and meticulous portrait of a girl, showing a high-bridged nose, a prominent facial contour, and a curvaceous body. We feel above all the dubious allure of height.

A topographic (relief) map of Hong Kong drawn up by Lieutenant Collinson in 1845 was the first map of Hong Kong to use contour, and it was also one of the earliest contour maps issued by the British Ordnance Survey, since it was only in 1839 that British military surveyors grasped the technique of regular contours to show topography. This is a set of four maps on a scale of 1:15,840 displaying the topography with contour lines marking every one hundred feet of elevation, but since it was in monochrome, the contour lines could not overcome the limitation of the flat surface to create a more vivid effect. In fact, transcending elevation did not by any means result from a determination exclusive to Westerners. In China, the "six principles of cartography" mentioned in the preface to "A Map of the Region of the Tribute of Yu," by Pei Xiu (224–271) back in the Jin dynasty, includes as one of its principles the concept of "higher and lower." Further, as researchers have pointed out, a kind of primitive contour lines can be seen in the Tang dynasty "A Map of the True Shape of the Five Peaks." Thereafter, however,

China was obviously overtaken by the West in the competition over height on paper and left far behind.

At the end of the twentieth century, the crystallization of the visualization of elevation can be seen in any topographic map on the scale of 1:20,000. By means of separate color layers, or contour lines at sixty-five feet vertical distance, and aided by the three-dimensional (shadow) effect created by the shaded-relief method, we seem to see the elevation of the surface, convinced that a place in the completely flat map has mountains rising to a height of almost three thousand feet and assured that there is a towering peak on this small island, with its area of only thirty square miles, with dense contours and steep gradients bearing witness to sharply rising desires and an arduous course of upward striving.

According to Hong Kong geographical materials issued by the Hong Kong Lands Department in April 1996, all land elevations are given in relation to the Hong Kong Principal Datum, and this datum is four feet lower than the mean sea level. Hong Kong's actual elevation is perhaps a little lower than the one of our imagination.

47

GEOLOGICAL DISCRIMINATION

From a geological map of Hong Kong completed in 1986 by the Geo-
technical Engineering Office, we can find clues about the exploration of indigenous culture that was supposed to have been ardently
pursued in Hong Kong in the 1980s and 1990s. In this geological
map (identified by serial number 11), whose scope covers Hong
Kong Island and the Kowloon Peninsula, the geological formations
shown in the map can be roughly divided into four kinds: (1) igneous rock (indicated on the map by colors in shades of crimson),
which is concentrated in central and northern Hong Kong Island
and the main part of the Kowloon Peninsula and consists mainly
of semideveloped hill slopes, with only the original shore of Central and Sheung Wan and the area of Tsim Sha Tsui developed
into central urban areas; (2) volcanic rock (indicated on the map
by shades of green), which is concentrated in western, southern,
and eastern Hong Kong Island, with its center in Victoria Peak, and
consists mainly of mountainous land unsuitable for development;
(3) sediment (indicated on the map by shades of light gray), which
includes sedimentary rock, gravel, silt, and clay, which is distributed along the harborside of northern Hong Kong Island and the
foreshores of the Kowloon Peninsula and has been developed
mainly into urban areas; and (4) rubble and landfill (indicated on
the map by irregular crossed lines), the main formation along the

shores of urban Hong Kong Island and Kowloon, occupying almost one-third of the total urban area.

As pointed out in a PhD thesis in the Geography Department at the University of Hong Kong at that time, "From Postcolonial Theory to Postgeology" (representing the peak of agitation for indigenous cultural exploration), cartographical circles, in the light of the chaotic condition of the local land surface created by rapid urban development, brought forward a proposal for getting to the source by laying bare the intrinsic nature of geography. The timely completion of geological maps of Hong Kong has indeed helped us to discover the channels hidden underneath urban formations and to reflect on the implications of developmental tendencies. Cartography thus turned into a brand-new category of cultural studies, and the art of map reading became a competitive skill in study and practice among cultural studies researchers. Among different kinds of maps, geological maps are obviously most suitable for making all kinds of comparisons that are ingenious, exaggerated, and yet not lacking in internal logic, since the term "indigenous" in Chinese means literally "native soil," which in turn signifies roughly the "substance of the earth" or "geology" in Chinese.

The arguments of the indigenous chauvinists are focused on the distribution and relative position of different geological strata. From this perspective, the establishment of the city of Victoria, that is, the growth of local culture, was not built on igneous rock and volcanic rock from the distant past (from the Jurassic to the Cretaceous periods) but on comparatively recent sediment, even reclaimed land less than a hundred years old. Igneous rock and volcanic rock were distributed on plane surfaces at the margins of urban areas and on elevated rough ground belonging to the category of wasteland, unsuitable for housing and not much good either for cultivation. Earth used for reclamation, in contrast, although it is not a naturally occurring substance, can give rise to a unique ecosystem out of artificial materials; this is a phenomenon that cannot be lightly written off. Since the constituents of reclamation material are heterogeneous, including all kinds of organic and inorganic materials such as soil, gravel, and refuse, indigenous chauvinists like to stress its hybridity, claiming it to be a special characteristic of being "indigenous."

However, the meaning of signs can actually be reversed following changes in reading strategies. At the end of the 1990s there appeared a group of cultural studies map readers known as the Granite school who upheld the preservation of tradition, namely, the long-standing and well-established historical value of granite (a kind of igneous rock). Targeting the flat-surface viewpoint of indigenous chauvinism, they emphasize a vertical and historical excavation, presenting rock strata in three-dimensional sections and thereby exposing granite as the vast foundation at the deepest underground level. As well, the solidity and density of granite and the glittering crystals it embeds gain their unreserved praise. The rock cover on the earth's surface, which is loose, fragile, and subject to erosion, will eventually collapse and disappear under the unrelenting onslaught of time, while granite will fearlessly stand its ground, impervious to wind and rain. In contrast to granite, as mighty as mother earth in all her majesty, the little heap of piled-up earth along the shore will turn into margins within margins even less negligible than negligible. Not even a product of some geologic period, it is just a junkyard formed out of dumped waste material within just a hundred years. What kind of "roots" could we hope to find beneath this "native soil"?

In the indistinct rumbling at the earth's deepest strata, in the underfoot vibrations of faint enquiry, indigenous chauvinist map readers still diligently trace the chronological growth rings of urban shoreline reclamation on geological maps: 1985, 1982, 1964, 1904, 1863.

NORTH-ORIENTED DECLINATION

If we view maps as the perplexed expression of people's search for direction and their own position, then it follows that we believe the directional indicator on a map is like the North Star, indicating by its radiance (which although not necessarily overwhelmingly lustrous is nonetheless honest and reliable) the road leading to existence or extinction to each person who has gone astray. In fact, in the history of cartography, directional signs or compass images have taken magnificent forms, bestowed on them by cartographers blessed with a vivid imagination, such as star shapes, spearheads, or ship's anchors; but decorativeness in the symbols on local maps has gradually been replaced by functionalism, and compasses have been reduced to uniform arrows.

When we set free what remains of our historical imagination, then it is not hard to perceive how "The Outer Approaches to Hong Kong," produced by the British Institute of Hydrology in 1990, presented in a timely fashion a period of disorientation as experienced in this locality. Searching for orientation in a state of disorientation is in fact no different from adjusting oneself after losing one's balance in a global magnetic field, and this kind of adjustment needs realization precisely through systematic surveying and planning, in order to comfort those who lose their way in their journey through time and space. This waterways map assembled many years of British and Chinese government survey materials from the region surrounding Hong Kong and clearly outlined water-based movements into and out of Hong Kong, as well as various barriers, in a topographical map on the scale of 1:50,000 prepared by the Survey and Mapping Office of the Hong Kong Lands Department. In this map, which is drawn to a Mercator projection along a transversal axis, our attention is unavoidably caught by two directional signs, one on the sea surface southeast of Hong Kong Island and the other on the Pearl River estuary to the west of Lantao Island. These are both directional signs read in degrees, using large circular signs divided into 360 degrees, within which the needle points toward magnetic north.

Cultural anthropologists have pointed out that the composition of symbols in maps and their explanation are the result of observing and narrating reality, but it might be better to say that they are the projection of a given society's collective consciousness. From this perspective, some map readers consider that the ulterior title of "The Outer Approaches to Hong Kong" is "The Outer Approaches to China." Its real purpose is to explore possible entry points from Hong Kong on the outside to the mainland on the inside, and these shipping lanes must be north oriented. Therefore the direction signs are also a guide for the Hong Kong region to gaze up at the Pole Star, and what the compass points to is a destination to which consciousness strives. But what is obvious and easily seen is that the compass and the meridian lines in the rectangular grid are not aligned, and the degree number indicated is not actually true north (i.e., zero degrees). It can be seen from the map that the position of the Hong Kong region with respect to magnetic north deviates by 2.05 degrees to the west of true north. This is explained in geography as due to the declination between the two true poles (i.e., the earth's axis and the northern and southern points where it meets the earth's surface) and the two magnetic poles (i.e., the north and south points indicated by a compass under the influence of the earth's magnetic field); and this declination can also be seen from the fact that the true meridian lines through the true pole and the magnetic meridian lines through the magnetic pole do not overlap. For the same reason, a locality's true position and magnetic position will naturally differ.

Cultural anthropologists have read all kinds of possibilities into the narrow 2.05 degree angle declination between true north and magnetic north, which can be roughly divided into two schools of thought: the true north school and the magnetic north school. The true north school insisted on the general authority of the true north pole in determining geographical direction, taking as its reason the longitude and latitude positions on maps both being determined by the true north pole, and also the true north pole's position being determined by astronomical observations. This school maintained that true north pole orientation was in the orthodox tradition of "beholding the model in heaven and adopting the model from earth," while the magnetic field's erratic and unstable pull reflected in the magnetic north pole thus was due to harmful external interference. The magnetic north school, for its part, put forward an opposing opinion on the question of orthodox tradition; its adherents believed that the magnetic field's internal attraction was closer to the principle of intrinsic quality than the external limits of the earth's movement were, and that the attraction itself is the concrete manifestation of the dominance of magnetic north. Magnetic north is the hidden, intangible, intrinsic, and effective guiding spiritual strength; it is the ultimate destination of the north-oriented attachment, although this "destination" is in fact nonexistent. From this point of view, true north is by no means true.

Some radical map reformers challenged the grounds on which map direction signs pointed north. They believed it reflected how the history of cartography and the history of the evolution of human civilization conspired to rationalize the hugely disparate and unevenly distributed power between north and south. Apart from proposing a south-oriented compass as a counterstrategy, the reformers also advocated omnidirectional pluralism in cartography (for example, taking south as up and north as down, or east as up and west as down), the reason being very simple—there is no distinction in natural logic between up and down in the globe itself. In an omnidirectional field of vision, any kind of debate on the north-oriented declination in Hong Kong's waterways is itself a kind of declination.

49

THE TRAVEL OF NUMBERS

Archaeologists have made an attempt to re-create Hong Kong's urban appearance on the basis of a tourist map dated 1997. The map marks the main tourist attractions, such as scenic spots, art galleries, museums, open-air markets, entertainment areas, parks, and communication facilities, using numbered red circles; further, green circles show cinemas and theaters, and blue ones show hotels. Since tourist maps cover the main cityscape, representing a mode of that city's self-imaging and also carrying value judgments in regard to its geographical landmarks, archaeologists believe that tourist maps can to some degree reflect the true circumstances of a place. Using simulation software, they have reconstructed this twentieth-century urban space along the lines of the tourist map; what is more, they have also built a re-creation on the same scale as the original on a broad stretch of desert, in which the harbor area is replaced by sandy desert owing to the lack of water.

We can easily see at a glance how the circles in different colors are distributed on the map. On Hong Kong Island, the red circles are concentrated in Central District and Sheung Wan, including the Man Mo Temple (36), Cat Street (85), the old Sheung Wan street market (64), Lan Kwai Fong (26), City Hall (7), the Legislative Council (27) and Government House (13). The distribution of red circles in Kowloon is comparatively sparse, lying mainly in Tsim

Sha Tsui and along Nathan Road; they include the old Railway Clock Tower (8), the Cultural Center (16), the Art Museum (72), the Space Museum (81), the Science Museum (79), the Museum of History (75), Temple Street (90), and the Ladies' Market (87). The blue circles, which outnumber the red ones, are most densely located between Admiralty and Causeway Bay on Hong Kong Island and in Tsim Sha Tsui in Kowloon. The map also shows "buildings of use to tourists" marked in purple, with roughly the same distribution as above.

One person who had gone by plane to the interior to take part in the urban restoration tour made the following notes:

After we arrived at our destination, we stayed at the Peninsula Hotel in Tsim Sha Tsui, having heard that it was one of the oldest and most highly ranked hotels in the city's history. Looking out from the hotel window, apart from Victoria Harbor (paved with sand), we saw an area for cultural activities occupying the harbor front and a mass of hotels towering like a forest on all sides. All the hotel buildings rose from flat ground with nothing in the space between them, so that from a distance it looked like a city of hotels, with only a few so-called scenic spots and historical sites squatting between them. The next day the tour took us aboard a large coach resembling a ferry to cross the "harbor" to Cat Street in Central on the "opposite shore," for sightseeing and shopping for replicas of heritage objects from the city's past: for example, broken plastic and metal toys, moldy faded martial arts novels with missing pages and pornographic magazines, nonfunctioning transistor radios, electric fans and typewriters, corroded copper kettles, tarnished silver ornaments, makeup cases made of rotten wood, out-of-date calendars, pocket watches that had stopped, and tattered and torn maps. We all returned loaded with purchases. In the afternoon we made another frantic shopping trip to the authentic atmosphere of Temple Street and the Ladies' Market in Kowloon. On the way we observed that the only people we saw in the streets apart from tourists were people who served in the tourist industry. We did not see anyone playing the role of residents (whether this was due to a management oversight or what, it was not clear), but it is hard to imagine that this reflected the true situation of the city in those years. The high-rise hotel towers in the evening sun were like lonely leafless trees in the wilderness, and we seemed to be walking from (8) to (16) and on to (75) on an extremely simplified tourist map on a scale of 1:1, searching for the sights that had been arranged for us beforehand, imitating the past that had been arranged for us in advance. We came to a profound realization that this was a city that belonged completely to tourists, and, for this reason, we were also in the end obliged to leave bearing with us the tourist's easily satisfied greed and quickly exhausted curiosity.

50

THE TOMB OF SIGNS

The only intact set of Hong Kong digital map materials still in existence is the one purchased by a businessman in 1997 from the Information Center of the Lands Department's Survey and Mapping
Office. This set of materials is based on more than three thousand
geomorphological map sheets on a scale of 1:1,000 resulting from
surveys from the 1970s on and frequently updated and revised, so
as to follow up geomorphological changes with the greatest speed.

The main advantage of this set of digital maps is that it can
simultaneously mark different landform material using more
than eighty signs. In addition, users can make selective searches;
for example, an automatic search for a facility or specific type of
land or outstanding topographical and geological features. Users
can also select different scales and sizes, adjusting at will the complexity of the material to suit different needs. Each different category of materials on the map is delineated in different colors, so
that when it is set at full-screen display, the digital map becomes
crisscrossed by neon lights in all shades and hues. Compared with
traditional drawings on paper or printed plates, digital maps are
beyond doubt the crystallization of an unrivaled assembly of information at a superlative height of efficiency, but along with their
profound subtlety in categorization, digital maps, because of the
complexity of their information and the extreme simplification of

their signs, also give the impression of lacking differentiation and tending toward abstraction in terms of their visual appearance. In traditional maps we see the world in microcosm, but what we see in digital maps are colors and lines. The imaginative connection between the semantic complement of signs and their intention has been utterly destroyed.

Digital maps, compared with the great quantity of maps produced as material objects, demolish the mythology of maps to an even more advanced extent. From ancient times up to the "Comprehensive Atlas of Imperial Territory" drawn up on the orders of the Kangxi emperor of the Qing dynasty, maps were even kept hidden from view in the Palace Treasury, completely inaccessible to the public. On the one hand, maps were a tool of political control at the exclusive disposal of the emperor, while on the other hand as unique material objects in themselves they were symbols of power. Maps seem to bear a mysterious strength: to possess a map is to possess a kind of embodiment of the world. Digital maps, lacking materiality, have dissolved this sense of mystery; they hint at the world but they cannot possess it or pass it on, because our control over the world is no more than dots and lines and colors made up of computing bits without substance, and these dots and lines and colors can develop into different forms and shapes at the users' needs and whims. The user in manipulating the program continues by other means the ancient illusory desire to be in charge of the world.

The businessman who had bought the digital map created and confirmed his own kingdom every day on his computer. Shortly before his death, he invited a famous geomancer to find him an auspicious site for his grave in the land he owned. After consulting the businessman's digital map, the geomancer expressed himself as follows:

Sir, I cannot find any difference between one place and another on this surface. The five hues and six colors of these lines are completely foreign to the principles by which yin, yang, and the five elements engender and conquer one another. Be assured, nonetheless, that there is nothing that can place a restraint on your destiny. Since there is no place on the map that does not belong to you, I can arrange the most auspicious site on the map for you in accordance with your wishes. What you, sir, possess is the full color spectrum of the bits; what I design for you is the eternal vault of the signs.

The businessman possessed all there was on the digital map; he also lost all there was.

5-1

THE ORBIT OF TIME

Map archaeologists discovered in a book entitled *The 1997 Hong Kong Street Directory & Guide* a map that traces the orbit of time. This discovery delivered a ground-shaking tremor in regard to the firmly established concept of maps as spatial representations. Behind all map production is an assumption of frozen time, and on the assumption of "an eternal present tense" the state and appearance of the earth's surface are depicted "at a certain moment of time." This assumption simultaneously repudiates time and expels it from maps. Even if a time-related notation were to be made on a map (for example, data on the year when an area was developed), it counts only as a written "reference" to time and does not view time in the same way as space by expressing it symbolically as a system of map signs.

According to the above commonly accepted knowledge, when you first read "The Hong Kong MTR and KCR Railway Map and Timetable," it is difficult to avoid overlooking the possibility that this map is a representation of time keys. In fact, as far as the majority of map readers are concerned, who are accustomed to the concept of irreversible time, this possibility is utterly fantastic. These maps show us the four main lines in the rail transport system: the KCR line (in black), running south to Kowloon from Lo Wu at the northern border; the MTR Tsuen Wan line (in red), from

Tsuen Wan in the west through Kowloon to Hong Kong Island; the MTR Island line (in blue), along the northern shore of Hong Kong Island; and the Kwun Tong line (in green), from Yao Ma Tei in Kowloon through the eastern part of Kowloon to the eastern part of Hong Kong Island. The red, green, and blue lines connect at Mong Kok, Admiralty, and Quarry Bay stations to form a circle, and the KCR intersects with the MTR at Kowloon Tong station. Thanks to the existence of a spatial concept of maps, we are ready to believe that the abstract colored lines that wind along on paper represent the actual city's transportation network.

By reading according to this "common sense," we can follow the running times and frequencies of the trains at that time. Taking the KCR as an example, the time at which the last train sets out from Lo Wu for the terminus in Kowloon is 00:08, the time at each station along the way is 00:12 at Sheung Shui; 00:14 at Fanling; 00:19 at Tai Wo; 00:22 at Tai Po Market; 00:28 at University; 00:32 at Fo Tan; 00:34 at Sha Tin; 00:37 at Tai Wai; 00:41 at Kowloon Tong; 00:44 at Mong Kok; and 00:47 at Kowloon. However, some map archaeologists believe that this map can actually be read in a different way. The 00:08 underneath the phrase "To Kowloon" at Lo Wu station actually means "To Kowloon at 00:08." That is to say, when the time at Kowloon station reaches 00:47, if you enter Lo Wu station and board the train at exactly that time, then you can make a leap in time and return to 00:08 at Kowloon station. Using the same logic, it follows that if you board the train at Sheung Shui at the same time you can return to 00:12 at Kowloon station, and if you board the train at Fanling you can return to 00:14 at Kowloon station. The nearer the station where you board the time-train is to your destination, the smaller the time gap as you go back. That year, the maximum conceptualization of return time was thirty-nine minutes, and this railway map is a graphic illusion of the return time. It attempts to endow time with a visible group of symbols in a situation where it is displayed on a flat space, namely uneven, random, twisted lines, a group of orbits going backward and forward. In reading maps we take our seats on a train to the past; with the prospect of a future threatened with inundation before us, we face backward in competition with time, striving to delay the arrival of the present.

Clever map readers have pointed out that in the circular route where red, green, and blue meet, the time traveler can continually delay the time of return because there is no limit created by a terminus as he urges forward the perpetual last train, moving in repeated cycles in a self-enclosed orbit of illusory time, going for thirty-nine minutes followed by another thirty-nine minutes.

Acknowledgments

The following chapters of *Atlas* have been previously published in English translation:

"Aldrich Street," "The Centaur of the East," "Ice House Street," "Possession Street," "Scandal Point and the Military Cantonment," "Sugar Street," "Sycamore Street," "Tsat Tsz Mui Road," "The View from Government House" ["A Government House with a View"], translated by Dung Kai-cheung [credited as Dung Kai Cheung] in *Hong Kong Collage: Contemporary Stories and Writing*, edited by Martha Cheung (Hong Kong: Oxford University Press, 1998).

"Spring Garden Lane" (erroneously classified as an essay), translated by Bonnie S. McDougall with Wong Nim Yan [Wong Nim-yan], *Renditions* 66 (autumn 2006): 111–13.

"Ice House Street" and "Sugar Street," translated by Bonnie S. McDougall, *Edinburgh Review* 124 (August 2008): 28–31.

"Ice House Street," "Spring Garden Lane," "Sugar Street," translated by Bonnie S. McDougall, published on the Web site of the International Writing Program of the University of Iowa, September 2009, http://iwp.uiowa.edu/writers/archive/2009works/Dung_KC_sample_.pdf.

The author and translators are grateful to the publishers for permission to republish these translations in revised versions.

Author &
Translators

Dung Kai-cheung was born in Hong Kong in 1967 and received his BA and MPhil in comparative literature at the University of Hong Kong. He now teaches part-time in several Hong Kong universities and writes novels and short stories in Chinese. His major fictional works include *Androgyny: Evolution of a Nonexistent Species* (1996), *Atlas: The Archaeology of an Imaginary City* (1997), *The Double Body* (1997), *Visible Cities* (1998), *The Catalog* (1999), *A Brief History of the Silverfish* (2002), *P.E. Period* (2003), *Works and Creations* (2005), *Histories of Time* (2007), and *The Age of Learning* (2010). His book reviews and literary criticism are collected in *Contemporaries* (1998), *Writing in the World and for the World* (2011). He has won several literary awards in Taiwan and Hong Kong, including the Unitas Fiction Writing Award for New Writers (1994), the United Daily News Literary Award for the Novel (1995), and the Hong Kong Arts Development Council Literary Award for New Writers (1997). *Works and Creations* received wide critical acclaim and was ranked among the best ten in the Annual Book Awards (2005) of the two major literary supplements in Taiwan (*Unitas Daily* and *China Times Daily*). It also won the Adjudicators' Award of The Dream of Red Chamber Award: The World's Distinguished Novel in Chinese in 2006. *Histories of Time* won the same prize in 2008. He received the Award for Best Artist 2007/2008 (literary arts) by the Hong Kong Arts Development Council. He joined the International Writing Program at the University of Iowa in 2009.

Anders Hansson studied Chinese at the University of Stockholm and later in Hong Kong; he holds an MA from the School of Oriental and African Studies in London and a PhD in history and East Asian languages from Harvard University. He worked in Peking as translator and cultural attaché at the Swedish Embassy in 1971–1973 and as a "foreign expert" in the early 1980s. He taught Chinese studies at the University of Edinburgh between 1993 and 2006. On moving to Hong Kong he was appointed editor of the translation journal *Renditions* at the Chinese University of Hong Kong 2007–2009. His publications include *Chinese Outcasts: Discrimination and Emancipation in Late Imperial China* (1996). He is at present chief editor of publications at the Macau Ricci Institute.

Bonnie S. McDougall is visiting professor of Chinese at the University of Sydney and professor emerita at the University of Edinburgh. She has also taught at Harvard University, the University of Oslo, the Chinese University of Hong Kong, and the City University of Hong Kong and has spent long periods teaching, translating, and conducting research in China. She has written extensively on modern Chinese literature and translated works by Bei Dao, Ah Cheng, Chen Kaige, Mao Zedong, and Leung Ping-kwan, among many others. Recent books include *Love-Letters and Privacy in Modern China: The Intimate Lives of Lu Xun and Xu Guangping* (2002), *Fictional Authors, Imaginary Audiences: Modern Chinese Literature in the Twentieth Century* (2003), and *Translation Zones in Modern China: Authoritarian Command Versus Gift Exchange* (2011). Her home page can be found at http://ihome.cuhk.edu.hk/~z105771/.